CHASED BY THE DRAGONS OF ECUADOR OMNIBUS

EVA WILDER

ALYSE ZAFTIG

CONTENTS

GALAPAGOS

MINDO

PUYO

CANOA

QUITO

GALAPAGOS

Book One • Galapagos
Chased
by the
Dragons
PARANORMAL SHIFTER ROMANCE
ALYSE ZAFTIG
WITH
EVA WILDER

MISERY AND LONELINESS

*A*lice was miserable.

The humid heat in the tropics had made her frizz. Walking through this stupid underground tunnel and slipping on the muddy cave floor had covered her jeans in mud. So what if this was the "Tunnel of Endless Love"? She wasn't feeling any love right now.

She hadn't had any breakfast, she was on her period, and she was ready for murder.

Her best friend Gabriella touched her arm. "Hey, girl. Are you ok?" Gabriella had a little wrinkle between her brows.

Alice counted to five. There was no reason to vent all of her misery at Gabriella. There would be no chalk outline around her best friend. She blew out a breath. "Yeah, I'm ok. It's just that I'm PMSing, hungry, and coated in mud. And my hair's an absolute mess." Those things combined together added up to a terrible day.

"Do you want a granola bar?" Gabriella gestured towards her purse.

"Thanks! I forgot that you carry those everywhere. I'll pay you back with a batido." Batidos, Ecuadorian smoothies, were the currency of choice for their group; they served as repayment for both money and favors. Alice felt better already, and she still hadn't eaten anything.

Gabriella felt around in her backpack for a granola bar. "Here, sweetie. Peanut butter and chocolate. Your favorite."

Alice opened it and ate it in two bites. This day was looking up. Still PMSing, but the chocolate helped. The mud could be fixed by a change of clothes. There was nothing that she could do for her hair — antifrizz products could only debiggify so much — but she wrapped it up in a bun with her muddy hands and prayed that there was a working shower in their hotel room tonight.

The rest of the group caught up with them. Catie bounded up to them. "Why did you guys go through so fast? It was really cool to look at the rock formations." She was looking at them with the eagerness of a puppy.

Alice avoided looking at Gabriella. Catie was sweet, but she wasn't really the best company. Her eternal Pollyanna ways were not welcome at this dark moment in Alice's life. "Oh, I have a little claustrophobia," Alice lied. "Caves don't work for me." Or something.

"Oh." Catie scrunched her nose. "I love caves."

"I'm sure I will, too, after I get out of here and see your pictures of all the cool stuff that you found." Yeah, maybe that's how you talk to little kids, but Catie was the youngest of their group. Such a sweet girl, but she would bound into situations where she wasn't wanted all the time, like a puppy who hadn't been trained.

Gabriella cleared her throat. "It looks like the tour guide is taking us back to the bus so we can head for dinner." He was ushering the rest of the group back towards the bus.

Catie rolled her eyes. "I hope it's not fish. It's *always* fish. I hate fish. Ugh."

LUNCH

*I*t was fish. Alice didn't give a toot that she was eating fish, as long as she was sitting down and eating something. Catie picked at her food and ate the patacones, fried bananas, on the side. She drank her mango batido, a creamy smoothie that was a brilliant shade of yellow.

Alice let the medley of flavors burst on her palate. The lemon really pulled together the dish. Alice loved ultra-fresh wild fish, but it was thin on the ground back in landlocked Indiana. Even with every bite savored, Alice still finished the fish in about a minute. At this point, Alice's plate couldn't be cleaner if she'd licked it.

Alice sat back. "I'm finally full."

Gabriella changed the subject. "So, Catie, who are you rooming with tonight?"

"I'm planning on rooming with Fitz, unless you guys want to get a bedroom for three?" Catie asked hopefully.

"Nah, just curious," Gabriella shot back. Alice couldn't imagine a worse fate than having to put up with Catie for an entire night when Alice was already PMSing and miserable. Joy of joys, she could also feel how tight the skin on her face was. She hadn't looked in a mirror yet, because she knew it would be ugly. She was probably red as a tomato from the sun. It looked like she would need to buy some aloe vera tonight. Their hotel in Canoa last month had had some aloe plants, but she wouldn't count on it in the Galapagos. She had no idea if aloe was endemic, and she guessed that it wasn't. The people in the Galapagos were picky when it came to preserving the native flora and fauna, because it was easy to upset the natural balance. There wasn't any more food, so Alice might as well get it now.

"Hey, Gab. I need to head to the store for some stuff. Walk with me?"

"Can I come?"

Alice mentally sighed. "Yeah, of course." What else could she say?

The three of them grabbed their purses and headed towards the center of town. The town was tiny, so it wasn't hard to navigate. Alice had a dreadful sense of direction, though, and she always needed Gab in order to make sense of where she was. One time, in Mindo, she'd gotten lost. That would've been understandable — she was a transient tourist after all — had Mindo been any larger than four total streets. The entire city centered on a single plaza, and the streets formed a tic-tac-toe board. After that horrible experience, which everyone ribbed her about, Alice made sure to have someone who had some sense of orientation whenever she walked anywhere that wasn't home or school.

Alice grabbed some pads, aloe vera, and a huge bag of banana chips. Alice didn't eat bananas in the United States, but she did here. Bananas were everywhere. There were tons of varieties of bananas, far more than the yellow Cavendish ones she was used to at home. Banana chips might be enough to tide her over for breakfast. Gabriella grabbed a chocolate bar, and Catie bought some sunscreen. The girls headed back to their hotel, where they'd eaten dinner. Alice and Gabriella exchanged a look. They'd find a way to ditch Catie before she got them to play games or whatever tonight with them. Last night, she'd kept them up until 3 AM telling stories about her life back in the States. Alice and Gabriella knew everything there was to know about her family, even though they'd never asked a single question.

They were met by a frazzled-looking Esther. "Oh, nena, I have been looking all over for you," she said to Gabriella. "I have just received a terrible phone call."

PHONE CALL

"*W*hat is it?"

"Your uncle has died of a heart attack. It was very sudden."

Gabriella sat down hard on one of the chairs outside of the hotel. "Oh."

"Your family has sent for you to return right away. I'll take care of talking to all your professors and getting your assignments, if you are coming back. The funeral is next Wednesday. You must pack. You have a flight back into Guayaquil, and then straight back to the States."

"Ok," Gabriella said mechanically. She wasn't a messy person, and they hadn't really unpacked their bags when they'd gotten to the hotel. All she needed to do was bring down her luggage. "I'll be right back."

Alice followed her. When Gabriella got to their room, she sank on the bed and stared straight ahead.

"Hey, are you ok?"

"Yeah, I'm fine. Just give me a minute."

Alice sat on the bed and wrapped her arm around Gabriella. Gabriella lay her head on Alice's shoulder. She wasn't crying, but she was very still.

"I didn't know he was dying."

Alice had no idea what to say to that. "Yeah, this seems like a surprise."

"I mean, he had diabetes and a heart condition, so I guess it wasn't that unexpected. But, you never really expect stuff like this."

Alice, under normal circumstances, would offer Gabriella chocolate. "Do you want your chocolate?"

Gabriella looked down at her hands. She still had the chocolate bar that she'd bought at the store. "Here. You can have it. I know you're always hungry."

That's how Alice knew that Gabriella was really shaken, even if Gabriella wasn't saying too much about it. Gabriella loved Alice almost as much as she loved chocolate, and they were best friends. Gabriella had the metabolism of a runner, though, while Alice had the metabolism of a tortoise. Gabriella didn't have to worry about gaining weight.

"Gab, I'll carry your stuff downstairs, ok? Just walk down whenever you feel ready to go to the airport."

"No, no, I'll take it." Gabriella got off the bed. She picked up her small duffel and her backpack. "I guess I should go downstairs."

Alice squeezed Gabriella's shoulder. "Ok." She followed her down the stairs.

Alice watched a taxi take Gabriella to the airport to deal with her uncle's funeral. Catie was nowhere to be found.

Thank God for small mercies.

Alice went back up to her room and opened up the banana chips. The chocolate bar was still sitting on Gabriella's bed. Alice said a quick prayer for Gabriella's uncle's soul, and she caved to temptation and ate the chocolate. Hey, it was good for people on their period, right? Chocolate had some healthy stuff in it.

Alice got ready for bed. She had to be at breakfast at 6 AM tomorrow, without Gabriella as her alarm clock. That meant that she had to set a series of 4 alarms 5 minutes apart, starting at 5:30 AM since she needed 10 minutes to put herself together. She would've needed more if there were boys around, but this whole trip was really a girls' trip.

BREAKFAST

*H*er alarms woke her up, bright and early. Alice wished that she could kill the chirpy noise. Gabriella could make Alice not a hateful zombie in the morning, but Gabriella was gone for the rest of this trip. Alice's eyes were slits as she brushed her teeth and got dressed for the day. She packed up all the way, too. She hated the way that traveling around the Galapagos meant that she had to repack every night and every subsequent morning, but those were the breaks. Rich people could afford to take cruises that moved them around at night. Impoverished college students could afford to stay in a different hotel every night and spend hours on a boat every day, traveling between the islands. Alice couldn't wait to get started on yet another day of sitting in a small boat surrounded by her classmates, with the motor too loud for anybody to actually talk.

Alice went to breakfast, and it was her favorite: fresh fish and bananas. There was a limit to how much fish she would love and how many bananas she'd eat. She only had herself to blame for the banana chips last night, though. She got coffee for fortification, and then she added a liberal amount of cream and sugar. She sighed and sat next to Catie, because she didn't want to be a friendless loser.

"Hey."

"Hi!" Catie was always 100% awake the instant she opened her eyes. "Aren't you excited that we're going to Floreana today?"

"Yes," Alice said, deadpan.

"Oh, you," Catie said in her chipper voice.

Shoot me. Without Gab there to save her, she was doomed to spending the rest of this trip with someone who was a bright little ray of sunshine in the morning.

The entire group went back out to the boat again, ready for yet another day of confinement.

Today was different, though. The boat passed a rock with tiny penguins, a lot of blue-footed boobies, and a pelican on it. All of us took pictures. A little way out from Santa Cruz, the captain exclaimed, "Dolphins!" Everyone crowded to the back of the boat to take a look, and the angle of the boat tipped sharply. "To the front!" the captain ordered. Everyone sat back down in their seats.

The tour guide, normally taciturn on the trips between the islands, shouted, "We can swim with them, if you want."

Everyone wanted to swim with the wild dolphins. Alice did not, and she watched everyone else strip down to their skivvies and hop into the water. Catie, ever sweet, looked at Alice, who huddled in the corner fully clothed.

"Are you ok? Are you coming in?"

"No, it's fine. You go, Catie. Take some pictures with that fancy water-proof camera of yours."

Catie frowned. She was a pleaser, and she hated it when anyone was left out. "I'll stay with you."

Oh god, no. "No, really, I'm fine!"

Catie gave her camera to Jade. "Take some pictures for me, ok?"

Jade nodded, and then she dove into the water, like everyone else.

"I'm not really a fan of treading water in the open sea, anyway."

Alice appreciated the gesture, but she would have much rather been left alone. The dolphins tired of the humans' company and swam away. She wished that it was that easy to get rid of Catie, but Alice was stuck in the boat with her and all the rest of the group.

Jade gave the waterproof camera back to Catie, and Catie oohed and aahed at the pictures Jade had been able to take. Everyone sat around wet, as there were no towels. They'd dry off quickly in the heat near the Equator, though. Alice saw that Catie really wished that she'd been able to get in the water with the wild dolphins by seeing how sad Catie was to miss the experience.

I have to shake her. It's for her own good.

THE GALAPAGOS AFFAIR

After another half hour, they arrived on Floreana. There were birds circling overhead.

Catie went over to their tour guide and shot him her indefatigable grin. "What are those?"

"Those are Galapagos hawks. It's funny, though, because they aren't supposed to be on Floreana. But you know how birds are."

Catie shrugged. "They're migratory creatures. They look pretty though, almost purple."

The tour guide frowned. "The hawks are brown. I'm sure it's just a trick of the light or the sun's reflection off the water."

"Must be."

Catie moseyed back to her seat next to Alice. "Cool birds, huh?"

"Yup," Alice said, although Alice couldn't have told you the difference between a starling and a sparrow. She was no ornithologist.

The boat docked at the island. Everyone got dressed, and the group headed towards land. Alice was the last one out, and the extremely tan tour guide gave her a hand. "Can't get enough of the boat, no?"

Alice gave a short laugh. "Guess I can't."

"You get seasick?"

"No, I don't."

The tour guide nodded, and then he headed forward to lead the group to Floreana. "There is a great mystery here, on Floreana," he called loudly, trying to get the group's attention. "It was called the Galapagos Affair. In 1929, a German doctor moved very far away, and he landed in the Galapagos. He was married, but he stole away the wife of another man." Gasps.

"Yes, it was quite shocking at that time. It does sound like a telenovela or soap opera. The Ritters set up a home here and became celebrities."

"They were joined in 1931 by the Wittmers, also German. But the Wittmers are not as interesting as the next group to arrive. The lovely Baroness Eloise Wehrborn de Wagner-Bosquet, an Austrian, brought two German lovers, Rudolf Lorenz and Robert Philippson. She was a beautiful seductress, and ships everywhere in the Pacific went to Floreana to meet her."

"Her presence irritated the others on the island, especially Dr. Ritter. Dr. Ritter began to fight with his lover. Philippson began to beat Lorenz, and he sought refuge with the Wittmers. In March of 1934, the sexy baroness and Philippson left Floreana. The Wittmers claimed that, prior to leaving, the baroness came to them and told them that they were leaving everything that they weren't taking with them to Lorenz. They were leaving on a yacht with some friends to travel to Tahiti."

"There were fishy details, though. There was never a ship that week. The baroness and Philippson never went to Tahiti, and they never showed up again. The doctor and his ex-lover believed that Lorenz murdered them, and the Wittmers provided an alibi."

"Lorenz needed to get out of Floreana. A fisherman named Nuggerud took him to Santa Cruz, and then to San Cristobal, where he could get a ferry to Guayaquil, where you have all been. After leaving Santa Cruz, though, they disappeared. Their desiccated bodies later showed up on Marchena. Marchena is to the north of Santa Cruz, while Floreana is in the south, near Española. If the ocean had pushed them back between Santa Cruz and San Cristobal, their bodies would have landed near either of those islands, Seymour Norte, Baltra, where you landed at the airport, or Santa Fe."

"And that, my friends, is the story of the Galapagos Affair, which has stumped historians. It was the source of a documentary made in 2013."

The whole group clapped, including Alice. It might be a tall tale, sure, but it did make for some good entertainment. You could say a lot about the guide, but he knew how to tell a story.

"And now, if you'll get changed into your bathing suits, we will go into the ocean again, right after you've just dried off and gotten dressed."

Everyone hustled inside to the bathrooms. There was no modesty — everyone had just been sitting around nearly naked — so everyone switched into bathing suits quickly. Alice, a little more shy about her curves than the others, went into a stall to get changed. She was the last one out of the bathroom.

When she got out, Catie came up to her. "Hey! Everyone else is already paired up to go snorkeling and has their gear. Grab some, and you can snorkel with me and Jade. The guide says that none of us can be alone at Devil's Crown."

Alice didn't like it, but she didn't really have a choice in the matter. Gabriella was gone, and the tour guide was an asshole who couched his snarky comments behind a veneer of concern for the safety and well-being of the group. The tour guides had to be natives of the Galapagos, and there was a shortage. As a result, the tour guides didn't really have to care about customer service. They would always have jobs, no matter if they got fired from one tourism company.

Alice put on her gear, and she went in the water with the other two girls. She lagged behind, letting her fins come out of the water, which slowed down her swimming speed. Catie popped up as soon as she saw that Alice wasn't keeping up with them. "Hey, do you want us to wait until you can catch up with us?"

"No," Alice called back, the water carrying back the sound. "I'm fine. Don't worry. I'm right behind you."

Catie nodded, and she followed Jade to go towards the sea lions. Alice slowed down even more. *Finally.* Catie was sweet to care, but she was stifling now that Gabriella wasn't there to deflect her. Catie had an underlying need for approval, and Alice, for some reason, was someone whose approval she wanted desperately.

Alice felt someone in the water behind her, but she was the last of all the ducklings in her group. Alice swallowed a mouthful of sea water, forgetting to snorkel properly, as she kicked away. Her mask was coming off, and she tried to lift her head above the water. For some reason, though, she couldn't rise above it to get air. Something was holding onto her arm. She fell down, down, down, and there was no one to save her. She shook whatever it was off of her arm. She saw the light above her, and she kicked hard towards it, hoping that the air in her body would buoy her to the surface eventually. Someone would find her, maybe.

That was her last thought before blacking out.

WAKING UP

*A*lice woke up to someone resuscitating her. *Thank you, Catie, for coming back for me. I owe you a hell of a lot more than a batido for this.*

She groaned.

"Easy."

She spewed salt water all over the person giving her CPR, which was little thanks for rescuing her. She opened her eyes. She was in a cave.

Where's Catie? Where's the group?

She began to panic, and she tried to sit up. Two strong hands on her shoulders pushed her back down. "Stay there until you don't feel nauseous anymore."

Alice stopped fighting to sit up. The voice was an adult male. The entire group was made up of girls, except for the tour guide. But, the tour guide spoke with a strong Ecuadorian accent, and this voice had a more exotic accent, one that she couldn't place.

She opened her eyes, crusted with sea water.

"Easy, now. That'll burn."

She wiped off her eyes and turned towards the voice. "Who are you?"

"I'm Castor." The gently rolled r at the end told her that she was dealing with a native Spanish-speaker. "Your throat must burn, but I have some soothing tea."

"Yes, please."

"I will help you sit up slowly, then. We must get all the sea water you swallowed out, but it does not feel good to vomit it all up."

His arms went to her back, and he slowly eased her up with little effort.

Alice felt as weak as a newborn kitten. He gave her a small teacup and white saucer.

"Sip slowly."

Alice drank it a little bit at a time. He'd added just a touch of honey, for which she was grateful. The dark tea was a little bitter and tasted a little coppery, but most of the time everything that was good for you tasted awful. Everything bad tasted great.

Castor watched her drink down the tea. "How do you feel? Do you feel ok?"

"Yeah." She was surprised by how much better she felt. She felt better than she ever had in her life. "What's in there?"

Castor smiled a little tucked-away grin. "Secret sauce."

Alice smiled back. She loved guys with a sense of humor. "Okay. Could you get me a phone? I need to call my group. Actually, could you tell me the address? Someone can come for me, and I'll be out of your hair."

Castor sighed. "There might be a problem with that."

"Oh?" Alice was a little scared, but she was a brown belt in tae kwon do. If this guy wanted to go, she'd go.

Castor turned around and gave her another cup of tea. He wanted to make sure that she drink more of the dark tea to settle her stomach. The taste of honey it was a little stronger now. The taste of honey was a little stronger now. Alice didn't know if she liked the taste of it, but she enjoyed the pretty little cup.

"Do you feel ok? Do you need to throw up?"

"No, the nausea passed after I first got rid of the sea water. Give me a phone. Please." Alice was a little irritated by Castor giving her more tea instead of reuniting her with the group.

"I guess we need to have a talk."

Alice raised a brow. "Ok."

"Your last name is Pinto, yes?"

"Yes. My dad's of Spanish descent, even though he doesn't really speak any Spanish. We only speak English at home, my mom, my dad, my brother, and I."

Castor waved his hand impatiently, like she was babbling insignificant nonsense. He was the one who brought it up, though. "You're a Pinto."

"Yes, and everyone always calls me Pintobean."

"I don't care about your nickname," Castor said slowly. "I care about your bloodline."

"My bloodline?"

"There are certain families which are more compatible with us than others. Certain families, like your line. The women interest us."

"Interest you how?" She was about 20 seconds away from knocking this guy out and running like the wind. She was lost nearly 100% of the time anyway, and she always managed to find her way back. It was a little harder on an island, but surely they'd noticed that she was missing by now and could send a search party.

"They…" Castor cleared his throat. "They make good wives."

That was enough for Alice. She went towards the door. Castor put himself in front of the door. "Listen, please."

"You have one minute to tell me what's going on, or I swear you will wake up with a headache for the next month."

GOING HOME

astor chuckled. "Sassy. We like that. You'll find that strong women do very well."

"59...58..." Alice was not joking.

Castor held up his hands. "Ok, ok. The short version is that you've been chosen to be our queen."

"What?"

"Whenever the old queen dies, she appoints a successor. We pull on the fate lines so that the successor comes to us."

Alice frowned. "I chose to come to Ecuador. I mean, I applied because the kid who sat next to me in Spanish class was Ecuadorian. He always made it sound like a blast. Beautiful and tropical. I thought that it would be a good escape from the Indiana winter."

"It is a good escape from this Indiana. You'll find that it may be a permanent escape from Indiana." He met her eyes again.

"Stop being a snotty know-it-all, and tell me what's going on!"

"You will probably live here now."

"Says who?"

"You have a choice, but you should hear it all before you make the choice."

Alice didn't trust this guy, but she didn't really have a choice. The door opened, and someone who looked just like Castor walked through it.

He was just as scrumptious as Castor, but Alice wasn't as concerned with that as she might've been back in the normal course of things. "Who are you?"

"I'm Pollux." He crossed his arms and leaned on the wall.

"Pollux. Castor and Pollux. Ugh, could you be less original with your fake names than to name yourselves after Helen of Troy's brothers?"

"They are not fake names, my liege."

"Explain why I'm the queen."

The brothers exchanged a look. Castor started. "The gift of precognition is given to our queen. As she grows older, the gift fades. On the day that she's crowned, though, she gets a vision of the end."

"Her death?"

"Her passing, yes. We do not consider those who have passed from the mortal world to be dead, per se. We know that they are not."

This was a little too much information. Great, they believed that people were undead. Too much weirdness was going on. "Ok. What do I have to do with this?"

"Because she was blessed with precognition, Marisa knew who her successor was. You were. We made sure to plant the seeds. Last year was the only year that Ecuador registration was open a month later than the other Spanish-speaking travel programs. Did you notice that it jived with your last-minute application?"

Alice was silent. Castor picked up speed, and he explained himself.

"We made sure that you were accepted, and we made sure that there were funds for you to go on the trips with all of the others. We're behind the scholarship that supported your trip here."

"If I stayed here — and I'm not even remotely saying that I am — what would happen to the rest of my life?"

"We'd send a simulacrum in your place."

"A changeling."

"Not as such. Changelings are malevolent creatures. A simulacrum would live your life for you. No one would look for or grieve for someone who yet lived."

"So if I stay, I get to be your queen. What does that mean?"

"You'll be our leader. Our society is matriarchal. My brother and I —" Castor indicated Pollux and himself, "we would like to be your consorts. That is your choice, of course." Castor looked deferential, but Pollux looked bored, as if her choice was a forgone conclusion.

Alice's eyes widened. "Both of you? This is slightly cliché, though. The virgin and the dragon. The virgin and the dragons." This setup was not how she planned to lose her virginity.

"You are not a sacrifice. You are a great gift to the Galapagos, and fate has brought you here. You can deny fate, but it will cost you." Pollux scratched his ear.

"Cost me how?"

"To tear asunder all of the pulling that we've done to weave you into this place would cause what mortals call 'bad luck.' You'd find that nothing ever went your way again if you left. Someone — a baroness — she was offered the position, and she went."

"Can't you just undo the weaving?"

"It's not that easy. No one can change the past. We can only make the future. In addition, touching the fate lines at all costs an enormous amount of magic. We've used all the latent magic to bring you here, and it would take time again to be able to unweave you from the islands."

"And if I stay?"

"You will wield the magic of the islands and rule our part of the Brood."

"Brood?"

"Our family. Our kin. Our line."

"You were talking about bloodlines before. What do you mean by caring that my dad's a Pinto?"

Pollux cleared his throat. "I'll be blunt. You can have our hatchlings."

Faster than Alice could track, Castor slapped Pollux across the face. "Tonto! This is a delicate time for her. Get out of here."

"No!" Alice interjected. "No. I want to know the truth, if I'm facing a major decision like this."

"There are certain families that can breed with us. Most human women cannot bear dragonlings. Very few can. Those blessed with the ability have abundant curves, like so." He gestured towards her body. Alice crossed her arms over her boobs and tried to look smaller. "Women like you are very rare indeed. We need to have babies in order to ensure the survival of our kind. We live longer than humans — human lifetimes are just a breath — but we do pass on eventually."

"So I'm like your broodmare? And you guys are dragons?"

"More like we are your studs. You can choose to mate with any of the Brood, but we hope that you will choose us. We know how to navigate the internal politics. Our gold gives us a lot of power, both in the magical and in the mortal worlds."

Castor took her hand. "I will take care of you. I swear it." He kissed her hand gently, and then he slid back.

Alice's head was whirling with all this information. "How soon do I need to choose?"

"You have until the sun disappears tonight to make your choice. If we do not reverse what we have done before then, you will no longer be human."

"What?"

"The tea — did it seem sweet to you?"

"Yes. Why? Is it some kind of magical honey?"

"It's dragon blood, freely given. It will turn you into one of us or be fast-acting poison, killing you instantly. But the cost is your entire old life."

"You gambled my life without asking me?"

Yesterday, Alice's biggest problem was Catie and how to avoid her now that Gabriella was gone. Today, she had to choose whether or not to walk away from everything she'd ever known, or she could stay in the Galapagos with the sexiest men she'd ever met as a queen. A dragon queen.

It was a tempting offer, but she needed to go home. She couldn't imagine never going home and seeing her family ever again. As sexy as the boys — dragons, she guessed — were, she needed to go back.

She shook her head. "You need to take me back. I'm going to call the program. I have to go back to my real life, not some magical fantasy where I'm a dragon queen." Real life was where things were sane, and the dead didn't walk.

"As you wish, dear one," Castor said smoothly. He opened a drawer, and he pulled out a pair of goggles. "We will fly you back. You will want to put these on."

Alice put the goggles on. She was a sight, she was sure, in her swimsuit and these ridiculous goggles so that she fly dragonback.

"In order to stay human, you'll need to regurgitate the blood."

"Throw up?"

"Yes."

Alice stuck a finger down her throat, and she leaned over the trashcan. She let go of all the tea that she'd had.

She walked to the sink to get some water to clean out her mouth. "Done."

She was going back.

LUCK

*C*astor pulled her outside. "I can't shift inside. It's like a very large umbrella opening inside of the house. Come."

He brought her to a rocky outcropping, and she watched his skin turn purple. His clothes shifted with him, and he grew bigger. Much bigger. When he was done shifting, he was the height of a small one-story house. He was magnificent to look at.

"Wow."

Castor knelt down. "Get on my back. If you come up my arm, you should be able to hold onto my neck."

She looked all the way up. Alice was nervous. She'd ridden horses before, but she was pretty scared to fly on a dragon. "Isn't there a saddle? A harness, or something? This looks really dangerous."

"This is the only way back. We don't have a boat. We don't need one." It was true. What use would dragons have for a boat?

Alice was resigned. She was needed back home, and this was the only way back. She climbed his arm, up his shoulder, and then to the back of his neck. She leaned down all the way and clung to him.

"Ready."

Castor took a few steps, and then he launched himself into the air with a few powerful beats of his wings. Alice closed her eyes as she felt the world drop away beneath her. She'd flown before, of course, in an airplane. But in an airplane, you generally couldn't just slide off the side into the middle of the Pacific Ocean. She didn't know if she could survive this kind of drop, and she had no intention of finding out. The way that every part of her clung to Castor would've been sexy if he was in human form, but as a dragon it was just like riding a horse. A sexy horse that could talk to you and fly, yeah, but like a horse. Pegasus. She giggled to herself, which was better than opening her eyes and seeing the wide open sea beneath them.

"I'm going to drop you on Isabela, but I have to do it carefully. When I descend, I'm going to be invisible. It is how we've stayed a secret so long. It's ok. You will still be able to feel me there."

Alice hoped so. "Ok."

The boat ride between islands took hours, but flights took much less time. In no time at all, she saw the seahorse shape of Isabela, and they were beginning to circle in order to descend. Castor went invisible, and he landed. She slid off of his back and headed towards the buildings she could see in the distance.

At that moment, the land beneath her feet dropped into the sea. Castor grabbed her with his claws up, higher, and they watched the land where she just stood get pulled into the ocean. Nothing was left.

"Oh my goodness. What happened?"

"Bad luck."

"Do you have something to do with this?"

"No. You do."

"Me? Why?"

"I told you that you'd suffer bad luck if you decided to leave. This is only the beginning. Because you have decided to leave, fate will try to stop you."

"My friends?" she whispered.

"If you want to bring the bad luck to them, then you can go back."

"So, it's not like I really have a choice."

"You do. You can keep trying to get back. I'd have to prepare, but I could fly you back to Guayaquil. You can get a plane back to Indiana."

"Would my whole life be like this? One calamity after another?"

"Yes."

The choice, which she had, didn't seem like a choice at all. Either she could ruin everything and everyone in her real life, or she could stay here without everyone she'd known before.

"I'll stay."

Castor was silent. There wasn't much to say to her. She had to capitulate. Fate made sure of it.

THREE TOGETHER

astor flew back to Floreana. When he landed, she hesitated to get move. "It's magically protected," Castor told her. "No harm can come to it."

Alice nodded, and she took off her goggles.

Pollux came out. "You decided to stay?" He picked her up with no thought of personal boundaries. He swung her around.

"I guess so," Alice replied.

"Come," Castor said. "We will give you our blood again, and you can rest. Tomorrow, you can meet the family. You can choose different mates, if you want."

Alice breathed deeply. Castor had just saved her life. Pollux was his mirror image, but she'd bet that he'd do the same for her, no matter what the cost.

"I don't want different mates. I want you both."

Pollux slid her body down, and he captured her mouth with his. He tasted like the best wine she'd ever had, an incredibly expensive vintage. He tasted better, and kissing him felt like warm wine slipping down her throat. Castor was behind her, and she could feel a gigantic erection pressing into her back. With both of them pressing on her, it was a little hard to breathe. It was a thousand percent worth it, though.

Castor was pulling down everything. Her swimsuit was gone. She could feel his bare skin on hers. Pollux was suddenly naked, too. Maybe clothing was easy for dragons to get off by magic.

Think later. Feel now.

Suddenly, Castor pulled her off her feet and detached her from Pollux.

He carried her back into the cave, like a bride over the threshold. Pollux settled behind her, letting Castor take the lead this time. Castor thrust his tongue into her willing mouth. She loved it when Castor was dominant. He tasted like the best chocolate ever invented. Pollux was pulling apart her cheeks. He began to eat her out from behind, which no one had ever done to her before. His tongue was expert, pushing just the way she liked it. She groaned in ecstasy.

Castor took it as a cue to bring things to the next level. He moved so that she had to take his dick into her mouth, and his head was between her thighs. His hand and mouth went to her clit, and she fell over the edge, just like that. When the fireworks stopped exploding behind her eyeballs, she opened her eyes to see that Castor was on top of her, biting her neck and breasts and leaving a necklace of bite marks at her throat and cleavage. She was flat on her back; Pollux was somewhere else.

The mystery of where Pollux went was not too long, however. Castor turned her so that they were both laying on their sides, and Pollux took back his position behind her.

"Do you trust me?" he asked, nuzzling her ear.

"Yes." Though she hadn't known them long, she knew that she could trust them with her life.

He pulled on her cheeks again, only this time he was heading for another hole. She tensed up and squeaked. Castor went back to rubbing her clit.

"Shh, my heart. It will be good. You will see."

She could feel Pollux rubbing something into her ass. She tried to relax, but she'd never had anything up there before. She was a virgin at the front and back doors.

"I've never…"

"It's ok. Just trust me. Trust us."

She could feel him work his thumb into her. It felt so big, and it burned.

"Shh. It's just the tip. It gets better once I get inside."

She was breathing hard now, stimulated by the pleasure Castor was giving her and the painful pleasure that Pollux offered. Pollux had worked his entire thumb in, and though it still burned and she felt incredibly stretched, she felt a little bit good.

"Good?"

She breathed in. "Good."

Castor took that as his cue to push his cock into her wet slit. She grunted at the sudden insertion. There'd been no warning at all. She could feel the burn as she stretched all the way around his enormous girth. The pain elevated her pleasure, and this was the most intense sex she'd ever had in her life. She looked up at his face, and she saw how pleasurable it was for him. Castor kept a slow and steady rhythm, and she went higher and higher, moaning in time with his thrusts. Her whole body was shaking with the force of pleasure. She was so full, but somehow she needed more.

Pollux took his thumb out, and he pressed something much bigger to her back door. It was slicked up with whatever he'd used to lubricate her hole, and he worked it into her bit by bit. She knew to expect the burn now, and it was distracting to have Castor plunging into her at the same time. Her eyes were closed, and everything happened in a blind world where she could smell and feel everything. The scent of the dragons, the feeling of Castor's bites, the pull and burn in both holes, the solid presence of Pollux at her back...everything was overwhelming. She felt herself spiraling towards the sun, and this time Castor and Pollux were flying with her.

Pollux and Castor set up a faster, more demanding rhythm now. She felt their rougher thrusts pulling her apart. When Castor pulled out, Pollux plunged in. When Pollux retreated, Castor advanced. She felt the fullest she'd ever had in her life. She didn't know if she could survive this much pleasure, but death by orgasm was a good way to go. Her breath was coming in harsh pants, and her back was arched. Her toes curled as the wax melted from her wings, and she fell swiftly down again, even stronger than the first time. Pollux and Castor both shouted as they spurted inside of her. Their seed filled her up and gushed out onto her upper thighs.

Exhausted by the most eventful day of her entire life, she slept.

DRINKING TEA

When she woke up, neither of the dragons were in bed with her. She felt clean, when she should've felt sticky, especially with how much semen she'd been covered in yesterday. Someone had sponge bathed her. There was a navy blue silk robe on a chair next to the bed, and she put it on and went to search for the boys.

She didn't have to go far. In the next room over, Castor was cooking breakfast.

"Good morning, dear one."

She smiled. "Good morning."

"Did you rest well?"

"Yes, of course I did. I was exhausted."

"We knew. That's why we left you alone last night, though the mating takes a bit more time."

"More time?" She was surprised. "How much more time?"

"In order for us to be considered your consorts, we have to have a couple things. One, an exchange of, ahem, bodily fluids, which we have already done. Two, an exchange of blood, which we can do now. Three, a ceremony where we vow to spend the rest of our mortal lives together. Three requires a full moon, and you have to have the other two steps before then."

"So give me your blood, then," Alice said coolly, with a confidence that she didn't actually feel.

Castor laughed. "So eager. Ok." He turned off the stove. He took a knife and dug the point of it into his arm. A drop of blood came out, and he put it into a cup. He poured hot tea into it from a steaming kettle. "And you." He handed her the knife.

Was she really doing this? She hadn't known this guy for a week, and already she was taking a blood oath to him and his twin brother for the rest of their mortal lives.

"Brother," Pollux called, coming into the room. "You've started without me."

"You can have the knife after her."

Alice cut her self, a shallow cut with just a tiny bit of blood coming to the surface. She walked over to Castor to put it in the tea cup. Pollux wasted no time in cutting himself, careless enough to bring out more than a few drops. He flung them into the tea cup.

"Ladies first." She drank the cup with their blood in it. She passed it to Castor, who drank, and Castor gave it to Pollux, who finished the whole cup.

Alice felt an enormous sense of contentment and completion, as if being mated to them was something she'd been waiting for her whole life. The feeling exploded through her, and she felt like she orgasmed again. When she opened her eyes, both brothers had their eyes closed with the same blissful look on their faces.

"And that, my dear one, takes us most of the way to mated. Now, we must wait for the full moon to complete the ceremony." Castor flicked his hand, and a perfect image of Alice walked out of the cave.

Pollux didn't waste his time with words. Instead, he untied her silk robe's sash, and he began to lave her clit in a steady rhythm. Alice felt fire blossoming throughout her body, but Castor was behind her now, his hands ready to hold her up if her knees gave. She felt the fire burn hotter, and she gasped for breath as she rose and rose again. Her release ran through her entire body.

When she opened her eyes again, she was back on the bed. Both brothers were naked. "What just happened?"

"You blacked out when the fun was just beginning." Pollux dove in to start biting her breasts and soothing them with his tongue in turn. Alice wanted to run her fingers through his hair, but she realized that her hands were tied to the headboard with her robe's silk sash.

"I want to taste you, too." Castor pushed Pollux off to the side, and he knelt between her thighs. He was different from Pollux, with his mouth all over. He bit her thigh, licked her clit, pushed his tongue inside of her, and she came again.

Pollux moved his magical mouth to hers, and he slipped inside of her. He kissed her roughly and pulled her hair. He pulled away from her, and he put his legs on either side of her shoulders. She knew what he wanted, but she decided to tease him the best way that she could when her hands were tied. She turned her head to lick his balls, when he clearly wanted her to suck his dick. She bit his upper thigh to show him that even if she was bound, she was still in control here. He was breathing hard, and she felt the tension in his thighs. She knew he was close to release.

Her tongue went to gently tease the tip and drink up his precum. Pollux didn't wait for her to be ready, though. He shoved his dick into her open mouth and began to thrust towards her throat.

Castor had her legs spread now, and he was teasing her with his tip while rubbing her clit. He thrust three fingers inside of her, preparing her.

"You're so wet." Castor pushed in halfway, before pulling out. He moved in a little deeper with each thrust, but he wouldn't give her all of it.

Pollux was nowhere near as delicate with her. He raced towards his release, and she felt his seed flood her mouth and overflow it. She felt the seed drip down from the corners of her mouth to her cheeks and the sheets.

Pollux withdrew from her, and he rolled off. Castor picked up the pace now.

"How bad do you want it, my dear?"

"Give it to me!" Alice growled. He'd been teasing her for so long, and she wanted to feel all of him inside of her again.

Castor slammed inside of her, so hard that Alice felt the headboard bang into the wall and the shock ran through her hands. She felt the burn of his girth stretching her past her limits.

She arched up as far as she could, and Castor was far beyond the control he'd exhibited earlier. He was going at her like an animal, no finesse now. His hands were on her hips, and he was pulling her into him with each thrust. The silk sash was getting yanked considerably now. As he thrust the hardest he had, he pulled her into him and shot into her. The sash broke.

Castor and Alice caught their breaths. Pollux pushed Castor off of her, and he turned Alice onto her stomach. He bent her legs behind her and put a hand between her shoulder blades, pressing down into the bed. She turned her head so that she could breathe instead of being slowly smothered with every thrust. She couldn't wait. Pollux entered her, and he pounded into her. Alice put her hands on his ass, pushing him in deeper on each thrust, and her head was thrown back in ecstasy.

Pollux put his hand around the back of her neck, and he pulled her entire body into him as he thrust into her. She was at his mercy, and she'd never felt so helpless during sex. Castor had tied up her hands, but Pollux was dominating her entire body. "Come with me," he commanded her. "Come now."

Alice felt her climax travel through her entire body. She and Pollux shouted through their orgasms together. She felt his hot seed fill her up. Her thighs were wet with her juices as well as Pollux and Castor's. She was still on her front. Pollux rolled her over, and he pulled her head onto his shoulder. He kissed the top of her head. Castor spooned her from behind.

"You are perfect."

FIRST CHANGE

When she woke up, both of the brothers were gone again. She was cleaned up. She found very large shirts in the closet, and she put one of them on. Her stomach was growling from skipping breakfast, and she hoped that Castor would figure something out for her.

He had laid out a feast for her. A plate held bacon and eggs. She opened a silver thermos. There was hot chocolate inside. A glass of orange juice was on the table, and with one sip she knew that it was freshly squeezed. A jar of Nutella sat next to a delicate, sugar-encrusted crepe with apples inside. She ate the bacon and eggs quickly, and she took her time with the Nutella-coated crepe.

She didn't hear the boys while she ate breakfast, as large as it was. She started to think about what could've happened to them. *Did they fall into the ocean? Did they decide, "Eh, she's not that good of a lay. Let's just leave her there and move on"?*

Alice's anxiety rose the longer that they were gone. She figured maybe an hour had passed from the time that she woke up, and there was no sign of them. They hadn't left her a note, and it wasn't like she'd taken a cell phone with her when she had nearly drowned. It wouldn't have survived the ocean.

What if I'm stranded in this cave forever? They've sent out a simulacrum already, so nobody will ever look for me. I'll be like the Baroness, lost forever. My body will rot here, and the boys will never come back for me.

She sat there for another 3 hours. When Castor popped into view, she could have cried. She ran to him and jumped into his arms. He caught her. "Hey. Hey. What's wrong?"

"I thought you left me."

"Never. We would never leave you. How can you think that, after what we've shared? We've mated for life, not for a few hours or days."

Alice wiped her nose. "I guess I didn't think about that."

Castor set her on her feet. He put a hand under her chin to tilt her tear-streaked face up to his. "You should always know that we care for you. We would never abandon you without a word." He kissed her, making sure that she knew that she was loved and cherished. She broke the kiss after a few minutes.

"Where's Pollux?"

"He's dealing with a situation."

Alice raised her eyebrows. He could tell that "The Situation" was not impressing Alice. He sighed.

"Our family wants to meet you."

"Oh." She sat down on the ground. "Oh."

"I'd rather spare you the duties of being queen until you get used to being a dragon, but the Brood calls." He took her hand and kissed it. "Pollux and I will be there with you every step of the way."

"I have no idea of how to be queen, Castor."

"We'll teach you everything, I promise."

Alice's hands were shaking. It was too much in too short of a period of time. Castor picked her up, and he carried her back to the cave. "I think that I have given you too much time to think. You'll be a great queen. You just need to trust yourself and trust us."

"Will they come here?"

Castor shook his head. "No. We will go to the Broodmanor. It can only be accessed by flying there."

"So, I'll be riding on your back again, then?"

Castor cleared his throat. "No."

"What? How else am I going to get there if you can only fly?"

Castor looked at her steadily. Alice backed up a step. "No. Oh, no."

"You have to learn to fly sometime, Alice. You can't stay earthbound like a human. You're our queen now."

"I didn't sign up for this! I just wanted to go home, but then the ground crumbled."

"I know. I know. Shh." He wrapped his arms around her as she cried. "I'll teach you how to shift first, and then we'll work on flying, ok?"

"I don't want to be a shifter. I want to be an earthbound human. I just want my life to go back to the way it was, where my worst problem was that my best friend was in another country."

Castor sighed. "I know. This is the position that destiny has handed you. In time, you'll adjust." He dipped her back so that he could kiss her slowly and tenderly. It wasn't about arousal or taking. It was all about burgeoning love and the beginning of their lives together. Alice could feel herself relaxing and melting slowly into him and the kiss went on and on. She knew that Castor was trying to ease her troubles, and it was working.

"Come on. Let's go outside."

"Aren't you hungry? You've been gone all day."

"I just ate."

Alice started to ask, but she stopped herself. If he wasn't telling, then she had no business asking, despite all the commitment stuff he'd just said to her. Their relationship was too new for her to feel comfortable opening her mouth. They might have great chemistry in bed, but Alice was naturally shy. That didn't rub off when she'd nearly drowned under the water.

He put his hand in hers and laced their fingers together. She was surprised at how good that felt. He tugged her gently towards the door. "Come on."

The sunlight at the Equator hit her square in the eyes. It didn't make her squint like it had before, though. "The sun doesn't feel too bright. I've always had to wear sunglasses outside."

"Of course it doesn't. You're a dragon. Your blood runs with fire. What is the sun but a giant flame?"

"I guess that's true."

He pulled harder on her hand. "Come." He took her to his launching pad, the one that he'd used when he had tried to fly her back to civilization. "Fly."

She looked down at the steep drop onto jagged rocks. "Um, I don't think so."

He pushed her from behind. "Fly."

She spun out of his range, and she walked away from the ledge. "No, thanks. I don't have a death wish."

Castor caught up with her in a few big steps, and he spun her to kiss her passionately. His tongue was in her mouth, his hand was on her ass, and a thumb was stroking her clit from under her shirt. She jumped up onto him to have a better angle to kiss and to grind on his erection, which landed perfectly between her legs. She pushed herself onto him. Even though there was clothing between them, she felt herself get wetter. She felt each pounding beat as he thrust up at her, only to retreat again and again. She loved this method of teasing, and she wiggled down on him and started biting his neck, with her hands in his hair.

"Mmm."

Castor suddenly jumped to the side, and she could see the rocks rushing past her as they fell to their deaths. She screamed and clutched him closer.

"Up!"

"Fly."

"I can't!"

"You have to."

She was five seconds away from dying a horrible death.

Four.

Three.

Two.

She was soaring low over the rocks with Castor still attached to her and closely held by her legs. She was much smaller than Castor's dragon, but she was much more nimble.

She laughed and gained height. She flapped her wings until the thermals kept her aloft. Castor let go of her, and his dragon pulled into a sharp glide before he came back to her.

"See? I knew you could."

"Race you!"

Without setting a destination, she used her wings to go zooming into the sun.

*A*lice was exhilarated by her first Change. Pollux came home that night, long after night had fallen. When he came into their home, she bounded up to him, ready to tell him about her day.

"You Changed."

She pouted. It was supposed to be news to him. "How did you know? Did Castor tell you?"

"I can smell it. You're a full dragon now."

"I am, aren't I?" She smiled at him.

He looked at her, a strange expression on his face. "I can't hold them back anymore. It's time to meet the Brood."

MINDO

Book Two • Mindo
Chased
by the
Dragons
PARANORMAL SHIFTER ROMANCE
ALYSE ZAFTIG
WITH
EVA WILDER

RETURNING TO ECUADOR

I was exhausted. After I went back to Rochester to attend my uncle's funeral, I'd had to stay at my aunt's house. I wasn't going to home to my mom. My aunt had a good relationship with me, but she was grieving. It was a downer to listen to her cry at night. She wouldn't get out of bed.

I hadn't been particularly close to my uncle, but I was close to my aunt, an island of sanity in the chaos that was my childhood. I made sure that the dishes were done, the floors were vacuumed, and the laundry was done. I sent thank you notes for all of the condolence letters that she received. I couldn't lift the burden of losing someone my aunt loved, but I could take care of the little stuff so that she didn't have to.

I was home for only a week, thank goodness. It was depressing to be around my aunt, who was normally a pretty little ray of sunshine. I flew back to Ecuador on Saturday night to resume my life, one that didn't involve sending a million thank you notes. The biggest problems in my Ecuadorian life were huge essays written in Spanish. Even though I was conversationally fluent, anglicisms always slipped out when I was writing. Essays in Spanish like a mosquito bite versus a third-degree burn.

While I was gone, Esther had all of my professors email me Powerpoints of the lectures that I'd missed. Because of my bereavement, they gave me an extra week to finish all of my assignments. I knew that I'd fall further behind if I actually lollygagged, so I did them all on the Sunday that I got back, no matter how exhausted I was from flying from NYC to Quito on Saturday.

My host family was very quiet. They worked, they bought food from restaurants, and we ate dinner in silence every night. That might not have been an ideal situation for another person, but it suited me. They didn't mind if I went out late at night with my friends, mostly Alice, and I didn't mind that they left me alone and basically only fed me. With the Internet and my laptop, I could be pretty happy wherever I was. When I came in at night, I was quiet and courteous to them. It was a dynamic that worked, and frankly one much better than the home I'd grown up in.

I texted Alice on Sunday night.

Done with homework. Should we go to the bars?

Can't. Rafael Correa passed a law saying that you can't buy alcohol on Sundays at this time of night.

Ugh. I'd forgotten.

Can I come over, then?

Yes. I'll tell my mom.

Alice lived in the apartment below me, which definitely helped cement our friendship. We went to school together on the same bus, and sometimes we shared a taxi. It literally cost a dollar to get from our apartment building at El Telegrafo and Avenida de los Shyris to go to school. It had weirded me out at first that there were no absolute locations in Ecuador, but I'd gotten used to being told that places existed at intersections after a few months.

I took my phone, put on my shoes, and went down the stairs.

MISS ME

$\mathcal{A}$lice already had it open and was waiting for me.

"Hey."

"Hey. How was your trip?"

"Sad." I shrugged.

"I can't believe you went through all your homework in one day, Gab."

"I had to. You know me. I can't stand leaving things undone."

Alice laughed. "I guess that's true. Come on. I'll make us some smoothies. Do you want watermelon or guanabana?"

"I can get watermelon smoothies at home. Let's make guanabana today." I'd never eaten guanabana before getting to Ecuador, but I'd quickly fallen in love with the taste. It was the perfect thing for a night when I couldn't go out and party with my friends. We were pretty tame, as far as partying went, but we had a lot of fun in La Mariscal at trivia nights. We went to Finn McCool's on Tuesdays and the South American Explorer's Club on Wednesdays. It was wonderful — nerdy, yes, but wonderful. Where else could you get free drinks for being smart?

La Mariscal was also known as Gringolandia, for a good reason. Most of the people in the district were white, and it was really a playground for them. The pubs charged gringo prices, which were twice to three times what normal restaurants charged, but the waiters and waitresses always spoke fluent English. I'd gone to Sports Planet for the Super Bowl, which I don't even watch when I'm in the United States. I found hundreds of homesick Americans eating nachos and hamburgers while watching large men rough each other up while fighting over the pigskin. There's something quintessentially American about beating up one another for a few seconds, and then both sides taking a breather.

On nights like tonight, when there was no alcohol, it was a dead zone. It wouldn't take me out of my head, still spinning from the rude shock of going home for my uncle's funeral. If I were home, I'd make smores on a night like tonight. Although Ecuador had chocolate in abundance, finding graham crackers and marshmallows were a little more difficult. I'd never thought of how important small comforts were until I went to a country that didn't have them.

Thank goodness for alcohol, which was universal in human civilization. Alice took a little bit of the host family's stash to spike our smoothies, and we took them into her room. We put them on her nightstand. Alice put on Pandora, and I sat with my back against the bed while she surfed around on her laptop.

"It was exhausting."

"Yeah?"

"I don't know. I'm not really good with grief. It changes people."

"Yeah, I'm sure it does."

I was quiet for a while. "I think that if I died, no one would really miss me."

"I'd miss you. I'm sure there are a lot of friends and family who would miss you. You'd be surprised by how many lives yours touches."

"I think that it would be a shock, sure, but I don't really think that anybody would miss me after. My mom definitely wouldn't, and my aunt's in her own world now, after her husband's death."

"What about your friends?"

"I don't really keep in touch. And really, you're the best fit I've ever had with another person. You know when to be quiet and when to talk, which is hard to find."

"Thanks, sugar." She gave me a hug from the bed, which could also be construed as a chokehold in other circumstances. "Is that ok with you? Do you want to change that?"

I didn't know. "I feel like there should be more to my life. I'm an honors student. I have a job. I do my homework. I have two majors, because I enjoy both Spanish and Psychology."

"You're a really impressive person."

"I'm not, really. I'm just getting by."

"That's how everyone feels. We're all just getting by."

I bent my legs, and I rested my chin on my knees. "I guess. I just feel like there should be something more, you know? Everyone when I was growing up told me that I was so special, so smart, so good at everything. And then when I got to college, the professors demanded more and more. I was in honors classes, and there wasn't a lot of positive reinforcement. I don't feel special anymore. I feel pretty average."

Alice laughed. "Welcome to real life, Gab. The definition of average is that most people are. You're a psych major. You know that."

"I guess." I looked down at the floor. "I just wish that there was a way for me to have a bigger impact, I suppose. It's like I've come into this world, and I'm going to leave it without any kind of footprint. I'll just die a quiet death and not leave any kind of muss behind. I don't even have a cat or fish that would miss me."

Alice slid on the floor next to me, and she put her head on my shoulder. "People would miss you."

"I want to do something. I want to be someone who does something meaningful, something that means something to a lot of people."

"You'll find it. You'll find the right place, and then it'll seem so easy and natural for you to have a high impact. I'm sure of it." She gave me a side hug, and then she went back up on her bed.

"That's seriously enough of me being maudlin. How about you? How has the last week been for you?"

"Good, I guess. I got lost in the Galapagos for a while."

BLACK HUMOR

I sprang up. *"What?"*

She shrugged. "It wasn't a big deal. I got lost while snorkeling on Floreana, but Esther sent out a search party to find me. They found me in perfect condition. They made me see a doctor on Isabela, and he said I wasn't even dehydrated, which I should've been from swimming in the sea water."

"Jeez, Alice. That's so scary. Are you ok?"

"Yeah, I'm fine. What was annoying was that Esther wouldn't let me out of her sight after that. I also had to deal with Catie." She rolled her eyes.

"Catie's such a nice girl. It's just that…"

"She doesn't know when to stop? Yeah." Alice rolled to her back to stare at the ceiling. "Your uncle was so inconsiderate, dying when *I* needed you." She was such a queen sometimes.

I laughed. Alice's brand of humor was just like my own. And yeah, it was black humor, but it made me feel better. "I'll be sure to tell him when I see him next."

"Well, whichever of us sees him first can tell him."

"Deal." I reached up to drink some of my rum smoothie. "Did you get any good pictures?"

"Nah, I didn't think it was worth the hassle. Catie has that waterproof camera, though, and she posted a million pictures of the Galapagos on her Facebook. You want to look?"

"Totally."

I got up and sat on her bed. She pulled up Catie's photo albums on Facebook, and we went through them together.

"You missed the part where we swam with penguins."

"Shut up. You did not."

"We totally did. There are really tiny penguins on Isabela, and they're the northernmost penguins ever. They are the only ones to cross the Equator, which runs through Isabela."

"No way!"

"Yeah, they swim on the cold side, which is furnished with water from the Humboldt Current which runs along the side of Chile."

"I can't believe I missed that!" I wailed. "Could there be anything cooler?"

"You missed the wild dolphins, too, but you can swim with dolphins anytime at Sea World."

"True."

I saw a million sea lion pictures. One was of a sea lion just hanging out on a metal slide on a children's playground. It was hilarious. There were tons of pictures of the water and of the sky. I'd missed parts where they'd gone through museums, but after a while, all of the Galapagos starts to look the same.

"I'm pretty much done." Alice nodded, and then she closed her laptop. "Do you want to play Bananagrams?"

"Yeah!"

Bananagrams with two people was way more intense than Bananagrams with an officially sanctioned number of people. We were both pretty good with finding new words, and we could beat each other pretty equally. Bananagrams was our thing, alongside no-stakes poker played with candy.

She got out the yellow Bananagrams bag, and we sat on the floor and played until her host mom called us for a late dinner. Her mom made chicken soup with mote, fried yuca with pan-seared Chilean sea bass, and banana cake for dinner. Everything tasted great. I'd noticed that the flavors were stronger in Ecuador than in the United States. Her mom was a better cook than their maid.

Their maid came during the day. She did all of the housecleaning, cooked lunch, did the laundry, and shopped for groceries. In America, it was the purview of the ultra-wealthy to have household help. In Ecuador, it was part of being middle class. The minimum wage per month in Ecuador was around $200 a month. If household help in the United States cost that much, a lot more people would have maids.

So, after dinner, cleanup was trivially easy. We collected all the plates and put them in the kitchen sink for the maid to clean the next morning. I was too used to the luxury of having someone take care of me. In college, I had to cook my own Easy Mac and take out my own trash.

Alice and I went back to her room.

"I know what will make you feel better."

"What?"

"A Taylor Swift dance party!"

I smiled. It was so ridiculous, but it was true. The wonderful thing about Taylor Swift's music was that it had a couple layers. There was the surface layer, the one that fools you with the happy beats. It made you think that she was singing pop. But at the heart of each song was some kind of despair, the kind that had made Taylor's career in country. That's what I loved the most. The desperation in Style wasn't evident when you just listened to it. Everyone thought that the music video was really weird, with the broken mirrors and all the imagery, but it was the best representation of what the song actually meant. If you took away the electronic dance music beat, the songs were just as sad as the country she'd had on earlier albums, like White Horse, Back to December, and Begin Again. The black despair that was worthy of Evanescence was what brought me back every time.

Alice put on *1989*, and we spent the next half hour and change singing along with the lyrics and dancing around like fools in her room. The rum hadn't hurt any, and it gave me a good sense of wellbeing, which was helped by Alice knowing the perfect way to cheer me up. I knew that it's weird that sadness and despair underlying a happy tune cheered me up, but it did. It reminded me of the Glass Menagerie by Tennessee Williams. He'd written a play, not a musical, and his idea of the underlying theme song was something that sounded like circus music but had the bitter taste of despair. That's what Taylor Swift's music sounded like to me.

I was sweaty and out of breath by the end. Alice had done a great job of getting me out of my head, but it was late. We had school tomorrow.

"I should go. I'll be by tomorrow morning to grab you so we can go to school."

"Later, girl." Alice walked me out. I climbed the stairs to my penthouse apartment. It sounded more luxurious than it really was. In a developing country, the penthouse was simply the highest level in a building without an elevator or air conditioning.

The school week passed pretty uneventfully. I caught up with all of my professors, and I turned in all of my assignments. They made soothing noises about my uncle dying. I accepted their condolences, but it was almost meaningless to me. I wasn't close to him, it was only important because of my aunt.

On Thursday, Alice came up to me while I was in the computer lab checking Facebook between classes.

"Hey."

"What's up?"

"Some of us want to go to Mindo again. Do you want to come with us?"

I thought about it. The only thing that would be there for me this weekend was a lot of empty time. "I'll come."

"Great! We can go tubing and ziplining again."

I groaned. "You know that I'm too short to fit in the tubes properly. They don't carry child-sized tubes."

"You were fine. It's fine. You just hold the handles the whole time. You don't need to be supported by your feet."

I raised my eyebrows at her.

"It'll be fine. You can swim, right?"

"Whatever. I'm in. You know how Marta told us last time that there's a three-day pass for ziplining?"

"Yeah."

"I think that we should do that, if we're going back to Mindo."

"Do you want to book all of our activities through her?"

"Why not? It's the same price, and she has the phone numbers of every-thing in town."

Alice snorted. "It's not a town. It's a wee village in the clouds."

"That you got lost in."

Alice blushed, although you'd think that she would be used to being teased about that before. The first time that we went to Mindo, she kept getting lost. I loved her. She was my best friend. However, she had the worst sense of direction I'd ever seen in a functioning human being.

"*Anyways*, as I was saying, we can just go to Casa de Celia again. You and I can share a private room, and the rest of the girls can go to that cool treehouse room that they have."

"Sounds good to me. Are you making the arrangements?"

She looked at me with a plea in her eyes. "I was actually hoping you would."

I sighed internally. I got a reputation in the group for being an ultra-planner, just because I actually checked where we were going before we leapt. I preferred to take the bus rapid transit lines, the Ecovia, Trolebus, and Metrobus, anywhere we could possibly go without a taxi. After having the excrement scared out of me by the head of diplomatic security at the US Embassy in Quito during the orientation I'd had within the first few days, I knew all about taxi secuestro. Taxi drivers would kidnap people and dose them with scopolamine, which inhibited memory formation and made them acquiescent. We'd been in a lot of taxis since coming to Ecuador, but I preferred to be safer than sorry. It had earned me a reputation of being the cautious one. It was a habit that had gotten me the nickname Tantor when I was kid. I still couldn't watch Tarzan.

"Fine."

Alice beamed. "I'll tell them." I thought that she hadn't actually thought it was a question. I needed to loosen up and not be the one who de facto handled all the details. I was always the guidebook. I needed to take more risks. It was hard, though, because careful planning was how I'd survived my childhood. Every time my mom went to the grocery store, I quietly took some of the nonperishable items and kept them in my room. Who knew when she'd go again? She wasn't a reliable person, and I was.

I'd been so jealous as a kid, watching other kids go to Dad's Club soccer and Brownies. Mom didn't care enough to take the time to take me to any activities. The late bus in middle school had been the only reason I'd gotten to join the soccer team. The money to buy cleats and all my other gear came from my aunt. As soon as I was 14, I went through the process to get a work permit, so I'd have my own money. I waitressed every hour I could at the local Buffalo Wild Wings. I'd had to quit the soccer team to work as much as I did, but I still refereed kids' soccer games on the weekends during the days when there wasn't a big game. My manager was in college, and she was wonderful and respectful of my need to go to school and also referee soccer. She let me pick up all the hours I could possibly take while having time for other things in my life. I'd made my way up to assistant manager at BWW, and I'd been able to transfer to the BWW in my college town. I'd been working there for a long time.

It was really weird for me to not have that constant in my life, the late hours, the rude customers, the regulars, my coworkers. I volunteered on Tuesdays and Thursdays at an organization, Ciclopolis, that focused on promoting bicycling, which had been my primary transportation for a very long time. In a crowded little capital city located in a plateau with mountains trapping in all the pollution, bicycling was the sanest way for to people get around. Instead of a mass conversion to bicycling, though, they had instituted pico y plata, which did not reduce emissions. It just meant that you were obligated to take a taxi to and from work one day of the week. The taxi drivers were happy about it, but none of the rest of the Quito natives were.

My volunteer work at Ciclopolis had provided my spending money. There was a special scholarship for people who went to a handful of developing countries who stated an intent to volunteer. Other people in college sneered at the idea of voluntourism, but I really liked the concept. It was a way to get immersed in the community, and you could meet people outside of the halls of academia.

Everyone else had Tuesday and Thursday classes. All of us went out of town on Fridays together, or we all stayed in town together. It was always one or the other. Even if a group of us broke off, like the group of the five of us going to Mindo, there'd be another group going to Atacames or Montanita. It got complicated with a larger group, so I was glad to have a group small enough that you could count it on one hand.

I called up Marta.

"Hello, Marta. How's it going?"

"Well. And you, Gabriella? You are well?"

"Yes, I am. My friends and I are planning on coming to your hostel again. We were wondering if we could make reservations for the five of us. We'd like your treehouse and the little front room you have."

"Ah, let me check to see if they are free." I heard the sound of pages turning. "Yes, we have not yet booked them. You may have them. Would you like anything else?"

"Yes, you did an excellent job last time of setting up all of our activities. Could you set up tubing passes for one day and ziplining for two days?"

"You are staying 2 nights?"

"Yes."

"You have already been tubing and ziplining, I know."

"Yes."

"Would you like something new? Are any of you early risers?"

"I can be. Why?"

"There's an ecological station with German scientists who will show you around the cloud forest for about $40 per group."

"Is it worth it? Is it a good tour?"

"Yes, it's very beautiful. You'll see everything that makes the Andean cloud forest so special."

"Ok, we'll book that, too. Could you split that cost 5 ways when you set up our tab?"

"Yes."

"We'll give you a down payment when we get there on Friday morning on the earliest bus."

"Ok, I will have everything ready for you then."

"Thanks, Marta."

"You are welcome. I look forward to seeing you and your friends."

I went into our classroom. I nudged Alice. "Done."

"You're a star." She beamed. "That was so fast. You're our travel agent."

"You could pay me…" I teased.

"We'll pay you in batidos." It was the currency of choice for our group. With fresh food so cheap in Ecuador, we ate luxurious three-course meals for $2.50. All of us were obsessed with batidos, and we sought them out wherever we were. When we made bets, they were for batidos. We gave each other IOUs that we often lost, but it was fun.

"Deal. Who is coming, anyway?"

"It's you and me, obviously. Then, Fitz, Catie, and Jade."

I made a face.

"Catie's going to be in the treehouse. You know that she's nice."

I sighed. "I guess."

"Anyways, pack your swimsuit and hiking shoes. You know that ziplining is a huge climb."

"Will do."

Our anthropology professor began the Powerpoint, and we shut up.

BUS RIDE

On Friday morning, Alice and I met heinously early in the morning. I force-fed her coffee, because she was always a zombie in the morning. I needed us to move quickly. With all of our gear, it would take a long time to walk to the nearest Metrobus station. I hailed a cab, and we had it take us there.

We took the Metrobus up to La Ofelia, the northern bus station. Most of the time, we traveled out of Quitumbe, the southern bus station that was connected to the Ecovia. La Ofelia was only for Atacames and Mindo.

Fitz, Jade, and Catie were there already, raiding a vending machine for candy bars for breakfast. They'd already bought their bus tickets, so Alice and I went to get two more tickets. While Alice and I were in line, Fitz, Jade, and Catie stowed their luggage in the bus, and then they boarded. After waiting for 10 people, we finally got to the window. They gave us a ticket, a boleto, and sent us on our way. Alice and I shoved our stuff under the bus in the compartments, and then we climbed up the stairs to join our friends.

Fitz and Jade were already dozing quietly in their seats. Catie was wide awake and bushy-tailed.

"Hey, guys!"

It was a mistake to drink that coffee. I didn't have to look at Alice to see her rolling her eyes.

"Hey, girl. Alice and I are pretty wiped, so we're probably going to sleep like Fitz and Jade."

"Oh, yeah, ok. I'll just read *No Se Lo Digas a Nadie*, then." We all had to read it for our contemporary Andean literature class. It was a horrifying and semi-autobiographical account of being homosexual while part of the upper crust of Peru. Part of the Latin American culture was a concept called machismo, where guys had to be as macho as possible. The American cult of masculinity was a comparable concept. Homosexuality was the complete opposite of alpha machismo, and it was frowned upon and shameful. His dad was a caricature of machismo embodied, while his mother was the softer feminine side who loved him and would do anything for him.

My host mom, when she saw the book, got upset that I was reading it.

Why are you reading this trash?

It's for literature class.

How dare they? You came all the way from the United States, and they give you Jaime Bayly!

That, of course, spurred me to read the entirety far before I had to. I was quietly sick of the homophobia rampant in Latin America, and it was an act of defiance to read a book that had scandalized the Peruvian elite and my host mom.

"It's so long," Alice moaned. It was over 400 pages in our non-native language.

"That's why it's ideal!" chirped Catie.

"Have fun." I settled into my seat, balled up my jacket, and pretended to sleep. I felt Alice lean on my shoulder, and despite the caffeine, I was actually asleep within minutes.

I could feel someone shaking my shoulder.

"Hey, guys! Wake up! Wake up!"

Catie was worse than an alarm clock.

"I'm up. I'm up." *Please stop shaking me, thanks.* I opened my eyes. Alice was blearily rubbing her eyes, and I could see Fitz and Jade yawning and stretching out.

Catie was bouncing up and down in the bus aisle. "Let's go, guys!"

It is too early for this.

I touched Alice's shoulder. "Move it, slowpoke."

"I'm going, I'm going." She yawned. "Tired."

"We all are. Get your A into G, girl."

Catie lead our half-asleep group down the steps, and we walked to Casa de Celia. Mindo was extremely small. There was a central plaza that was formed by four streets, two sets of parallel lines that crossed each other. It formed a tic-tac-toe board, and Casa de Celia wasn't far from the bus station.

"Hello, girls! How happy I am to see your beautiful faces!" Marta gave all of us a kiss on the cheek and a brief hug. "I have set up all of your rooms. You have towels on your beds. You will tell me if you need anything more, yes?"

"Yes."

"Good. Now, here are your tickets for all of your activities. You'll go to the ecological station tomorrow morning very early." Alice groaned. Marta continued, undeterred. "You can go tubing and ziplining today. Ziplining first, I think. I told them to have a truck here an hour after the first bus arrived. I'll let you get settled."

"Thank you," we chorused. All of us trudged to our respective rooms. Alice and I put on our hiking boots. We always brought jackets, because the cloud forest was pretty cold in the morning. However, hiking heated you up pretty fast when you were slowly going up a mountain.

"I'm going to rest." Alice lay on her bed to get every second of sleep that she could before going out.

I had snacks, and I brought them to the treehouse. "Hey, guys. Is anybody hungry?"

Fitz and Jade were in the same state as Alice. Catie was reading. "Oh, I'll take some Oreos."

I gave her my Oreos. "Anybody else?"

"No," Fitz moaned feebly. "Early."

I sat on Catie's bed and ate some Oreos with her. I checked my watch. Fifteen more minutes to go.

"Catie, do you still have your waterproof camera? It might be fun to use while tubing, as long as you have the strap on your wrist."

"Yeah! That's a great idea." Catie knelt on the floor by her backpack. She stopped. "It's not a good idea of ziplining, but I'll definitely take it along when we go tubing."

"Yeah, perfect."

We had enough time to go out and do something, and I wasn't going to stay in the treehouse while Fitz and Jade were half asleep. "Do you want to go to the store next door? It'll take less than 10 minutes. We might as well pick some stuff up."

"Yeah, let's go." Catie took out her wallet. We headed to the convenience store next to Casa de Celia, and we bought crackers, Kinder Bueno, and Pringles. I took the Pringles, and Catie took the crackers and Kinder Bueno back to the treehouse.

"Alice, come on." I started jumping on her bed.

"Stop it, Jeff." She moaned. "I'll rip your balls off."

"Aliiice," I said. "Alice! I don't even have balls."

One eye opened. "I'll rip your ovaries off?"

"One, I don't think that's the same thing. Two, we need to go. Three, that wasn't a threat. It was a question."

"Fine. Fine." Alice rolled out of bed. "But it's on you."

"Ok. Let's go out to wait for the truck."

ZIPLINING

When we went outside, Fitz, Jade, and Catie were already climbing into the truck bed. We were the last ones. The drivers sitting in the cab of the truck were twins. They were tall and handsome, with the cheekbones of male models. They were also surprisingly pale. In Ecuador, most people were some degree of mestizo, with a little indigenous blood and a little Spanish blood. As a result, most Ecuadorians had a light perma-tan for which New Jersey housewives would kill. Maybe they were German. There were plenty of those in Ecuador.

"All in?" called the driver. He had a sexy accent, light, but it was definitely there.

"Yes," I called back.

"Vamonos."

The truck revved to life. We bumped down the road. In the United States, seatbelt laws outlawed riding in the back of truck beds. It was surprisingly comfortable. It wasn't unlike sitting in an open-backed limo, if limos had wheel covers that dug into your back.

It took less than 10 minutes to get to the ziplining place.

They unhooked the back of the truck bed, and all of us climbed down. I was the shortest, but I'd learned to compensate for my height a long time ago. I was no Kacy Catanzaro from *American Ninja Warrior*, but I could handle a world that was just 1% too big for me.

The twins were standing at the side of the truck, staring at me and breathing hard.

"What?" I put a hand to my hair. It felt like it was fine in my braid.

The driver shook himself. "Nothing. I am Victor Abreu. It is a pleasure."

He gave me a double-cheek kiss, the kind that Europeans did and Ecuadorians didn't. It looked like I was right about him being German.

"I'm Gabriella."

"I am Alonso." The other twin bowed to me, and he moved in, too. I was expecting a cheek kiss like Victor's, but he nuzzled my ear and smelled me, instead.

"You are delicious," he whispered into my ear. He kissed my neck. It was subtle enough that the four others wouldn't catch it. My knees felt loose. His hair smelled divine.

Victor was already walking up to get everybody's gear on. We had helmets. Alonso put my harness on me, touching me gently everywhere on my body. "I need to make sure it's safe." He tugged on every part of the harness, from the part near my breasts to the part next to my ass. With my body warmed up, it felt like foreplay. I blushed at the thought. Maybe German Ecuadorians were just really playful?

"Let's go." Victor pulled Alonso forward in an very effective cock block. They looked at each other, with some secret twin communication passing between them. Alonso lead the pack, while Victor stayed in the back.

"I'm sorry about that. Alonso is very aggressive."

"I noticed. He seems like a nice guy."

Victor snorted. "I am the nice guy. He is my opposite, my twin."

I shrugged.

"We both want you, but he is much more obvious about it."

"Excuse me?" Maybe it was weird that Alonso would kiss me on my neck the first time that we met, but Victor was really bold in his own way.

"Could you not tell? We both had an incredible reaction the first time that we saw you. We each want to make you ours."

"I'm not a possession."

"No, you are a woman. Tell me, Gabriella, what is your last name?"

"Peres."

"Hmm, yes. Tell me, what is it that you want most in the world? If a genie could come down and give you your heart's desire, what would it be?"

Victor seemed overly familiar, but I thought about it.

"I'd want to be happy."

Victor nodded. "That is a good answer."

Was it? I felt like it was ambiguous. When I was in fourth grade, we'd talked about careers.

Someone in my class asked me about it.

What do you want to be when you grow up?

Happy.

That's not a real answer.

Victor didn't seem to think that it was a stupid answer to his question, though, and I was grateful for that.

"Come. We must hurry to catch up with the others." He pulled on my hand and started to run up the path.

The zipline course had 13 lines, and it started really high up, since zipping always went down.

"Let's do the crazy stuff!" Catie was saying as we caught up to the rest of the group. "I want to do Superman."

"Yes, you can do Superman. There are only two of us, though, so only two out of the five of you can do Superman on any line," Victor told her.

"I want to go first," Catie said.

"Good. I will take you." He climbed up the steps with her. He hooked her up to the zip line from the back of her harness, and he got on, too. All of the zipline instructors always wore special gloves on the lines. Fitz, Jade, and Alice were helped by Alonso.

"Do you want to do Superman?"

"Sure." He hooked me up. He put my legs behind him. I could feel his giant erection pressing into the juncture of my thighs.

He pushed us off, and we were flying above the top of the cloud forest. Everything was still misty, but I could see thousands of beautiful orchids at the tops of the trees below me. I was getting wet from feel him press into me, even though we were both fully clothed. The trip was incredibly short.

Victor helped unhook us. Alonso said softly, "Did you like that?"

"I think it's the best trip I've ever been on. I wish I could fly like that all the time."

Victor shook his head, and he took the group down to the next line. We followed that pattern on all of the rest of the lines, with Victor taking one of the other girls and then Alonso taking me at the end. By the end of it, my cheeks were flushed, and I was wetter than the cloud forest. I imagined that it wasn't that comfortable to have an erection for this long, but it was turning me on a lot.

There was a psychology study once with the idea of arousal and exhilaration. They made guys walk across a terrifying bridge, and they counted the ones who asked the research assistant for her number. The control group did something that wouldn't raise your heart rate, and almost none of them asked for her number. The majority of the bridge group. Yeah, I was incredibly turned on, but I didn't trust my body's instincts to make decisions for me when it came to boys. I avoided them for a reason. I'd seen my mom get involved with way too many men, and she'd neglect me when she was seeing someone new. I'd been too busy working and studying to ever have a boyfriend in high school and college, anyway.

I wasn't very experienced firsthand with boys, but I'd seen enough hanky panky that I knew it wasn't worth it. My friends always went through the cycle of meeting a cute guy, hooking up with him, and then breaking up with him for some reason. Sometimes it was as stupid as a tweet. Sometimes they cheated. I wasn't ready to be with a boy without a commitment. I'd done fine by myself for most of my life, and I had no intention of letting some guy turn me into a crying mess.

Alonso was changing my ideas, though. I'd watch my friends hook up with random frat boys for one night, the kind that never called. I saw the attraction now, though. Alonso was the sexiest guy I'd ever met, and it didn't hurt that he had an identical twin that could match him. I got the impression that in the contest between Alonso and Victor, Alonso had pulled ahead by a lot.

As they walked all of us back to the truck, Alonso trailed to the back so he could talk to me.

"Hey, do you like to have fun?"

I eyed him warily. "What kind of fun?"

"There's a club in Mindo called Tatumbe. Our friends all go there, drink a little, have a good time. You should bring your friends."

"We're going tubing today, and we woke up pretty early this morning."

"I'll make it worth your while," he promised.

"We'll see."

"We'll be there starting around 10."

"Ok."

"Do you want to sit in the cab with us?"

"No, I'd rather be in the truck bed."

"Oye," he called. "Does anybody want to ride with Alonso inside of the truck?"

"Me!" Catie climbed in. Alonso lifted me effortlessly by my waist into the truck bed, then he climbed in after me. I'm not a small girl.

"You act like that was nothing."

"It wasn't. You are the perfect size." He wedged himself against me and the gate of the truck bed. His body was so hard, and he smelled so good. I could feel myself getting wetter by the second.

We couldn't talk in the truck bed, so he put his hand between my legs from underneath. My legs were together, but it didn't stop him. He felt my muscles clench on his fingers, and he smiled at me. Nobody else noticed. I stifled a moan with his firm, slow strokes. I was blushing. What if someone noticed? It felt too good to stop him, though.

All too soon, or just in time, we got back to Casa de Celia. He let down the truck bed and helped me out, as well as all of the other girls in a show of gallantry.

"Tonight." It was a promise and a command.

"We'll see." I walked back to my room, and I could feel his gaze on my back.

e had a blast going tubing, no matter how short I was. The water was moderately cold, but I didn't care. It was fun just to go out with my girls in bathing suits and float down a river.

Afterward, we agreed to meet up at 8 for dinner. All of us hit the showers, and we met in the treehouse at 8 smelling fresh as daisies instead of disgusting river water.

We went to El Quetzal for dinner. We ordered. While we were waiting, Catie went to walk around the restaurant. She came back with a pamphlet.

"Hey, guys. They have a chocolate factory tour. Do you want to go?"

That actually sounded fun. "I don't know. Do we have time?"

"Well, they do a morning and afternoon tour. Do you think that we could do it after ziplining tomorrow? It's at 4.

"Ok, if we feel like it tomorrow, we'll go. I promise."

Catie's lower lip stuck out. "Ok." She sat down next to Fitz.

We ordered our food and settled in. Fitz was talking to Catie and Jade about how boring literature class was, while Alice and I were having our own private conversation.

"So, those guys…"

I blushed. "I know, right?"

"They're twins! Get'em girl."

I sighed. "I don't know. It's too much to handle. And I'm only here for the weekend."

"You deserve to let loose. This isn't like hooking up with someone in Quito or back home. Mindo is basically another world."

"I think you're right." I probably was listening for what I wanted to hear, but she was right. Mindo could be my Vegas. "I guess we should go to the bar."

Alice bumped my shoulder with hers. "That's my girl."

With a speed uncharacteristic of Ecuadorian service, we got our food almost immediately. I ate my chicken breast with papas doradas. It was weird that they didn't debone chicken breasts in Ecuador, but like everything else, I got used to it. It was nice and salty, and the potatoes definitely hit the spot.

At the end, we gorged on fantastic chocolate brownies made with the chocolate from their chocolate factories. The texture was really dense, and the five of us shared two. It was the perfect amount. When we were done, I sat back in my chair.

"Do you guys want to go out?" I tried not to sound too hopeful.

"Let's go," said Jade.

"The guide was telling me earlier that the best bar in town is Tatumbe."

"Let's go there!"

I'd looked it up in my guidebook of Mindo, although honestly a circuit of the town would've shown us. When we got there, I knew we could not have missed it. It was the only place in town that had loud music coming out of it. It was dark inside. In Mindo, there weren't that many bars, and this was probably the most happening one.

All of us showed our university ID to the bouncer, and he let us in. We staked out a table in the back with our jackets on it. Fitz hung back, while the rest of us started dancing on the dance floor. It wasn't packed with bodies, but most Ecuadorians danced salsa, which took space. If you weren't careful on the dance floor, you'd get bodychecked by someone doing some fancy footwork.

They were playing the newest Enrique Iglesias, and all of us were having a blast. It was as if we'd woken up late after a refreshing night of sleep. Catie was an excellent dancer; she'd been taking ballet since she was three, and she was the best of us. Alice and I made it up as I went, and Jade had this incredible innate rhythm that made all of her movements seem effortless.

Mid-song, I felt hands creep on my hips. "Hey," he said in my ear.

I whirled around. "Alonso."

"Are you enjoying yourself?"

"Very much. Where are your friends?"

"They, ah, couldn't make it. But I brought Victor." Victor was heading our way with cold beers in hand. He had three.

He bent down to shout in my ear. "Do you want one?"

What the hell. It was my Vegas. "Sure!" I shouted back.

Alonso rolled his cold beer bottle on my arm, and I shivered. "Do you want to go somewhere more private?"

Vegas, I told myself. "Hey guys, don't worry about me, ok? I'm good." I waved to them. Victor and Alonso parted the sea of bodies to take me outside. I just followed in their wake. Outside of the club, I could actually hear again. The three of us still had our beers in our hands.

"I've been thinking about what you said to me earlier today."

"Oh yeah? What was that?"

"You said that you wanted to be happy. Did you mean that?"

"Yes, I did."

"If I could promise you that you'd be happy for every day of the rest of your life, would you come with me?"

He startled a laugh out of me. "That sounds a lot like a marriage proposal."

He shrugged. "Answer me."

"I mean, it's hypothetical, right?"

"Sure." He watched me carefully.

"Sure. It's what I want most in life. The pursuit of happiness is a fundamental American right for a reason, you know."

Alonso broke in. "Do you want your beer? You haven't touched it."

I raised my beer bottle, and I turned around to face the two of them.

"To happiness." They raised their bottles, too, and the glass made little clink sounds as I hit both of their bottles. I drank my first sip. The coldness of the beer felt good, and it slid down my throat pretty easily. The beer felt kind of sweet. I kept walking, and they kept pace with me.

"What's in this? It tastes like honey."

Alonso scratched his ear. "It's, uh, homebrew."

"You mean the bar microbrews?" He hesitated for a second, then he nodded. "That's pretty cool. Doesn't the elevation make that hard?"

"I don't know."

"Oh, well, ok." It wasn't that important. "Where are we going?"

"We're going to our house." Victor drank another sip of his beer. "We have better drinks than Tatumbe, and it will be easier for all of us to talk."

In a minute, we were there. Mindo was the size of a postage stamp. Victor unlocked the door, and he let me go inside first. Inside, everything was coated in shiny stuff.

"Wow!" I was practically blinded by the bling in the room. "It looks like everything is made out of gold. Is this like the gold leaf in Iglesia de la Compañía?"

Victor took a long breath in. "Something like that. Would you care to take a seat?" There was a pretty couch with gold fleur-de-lis on a cream background. I sat down, and my beer rested on my knee.

"So, what do you want to talk about?"

"I want to talk about your perfect body, your scent, your eyes, your hair, your nose, the curve of your lip, the taste of your skin..." Alonso was coming on pretty strong, but I'd never heard prettier words spoken to me. Ever.

I smiled. "We barely know each other."

"We know each other enough. Would you mate us?"

"Do you mean have sex with you?"

"Yes, mating includes sex."

My gaze bounced between the two of them. Alonso had his hair tousled, and he was leaning back on his chair. Victor had perfect posture, and his hair was gelled perfectly. Both of them could have featured on the cover of a magazine. *Vegas.*

"Yes."

COUCH, BED, AND SHOWER

Alonso was on top of me almost before I got to the end of the word. He took my hands in his big ones and pinned them to the back of the couch. He gently bit my neck before parting my lips with his tongue and kissing me deeply.

Victor wanted to get in on this action, too. I could feel Alonso being pushed to one side, as Victor put his huge hand inside of my top. He pinched my nipple, and I jerked. His other hand went to unbutton my jeans, and he had to use two hands to get the button open. I was really self conscious about the pudge that formed when I sat down, and I tried to back away, even though there was no room. Lifting my shirt, Victor went down to kiss my stomach.

"You're so feminine." He unzipped my jeans, and he pulled down my panties and my jeans in one fell swoop. Alonso bit my ear, and I arched. He let go of my hands, and I put them in his hair, controlling the angle of the kiss. He didn't let me do that for long. He pushed my hip so that I was laying on the couch. He pulled off my top, and he began biting my breasts.

Victor bit the inside of my thigh, and I involuntarily jerked my hips towards him. "Patience, Gabriella." He stroked my clit lightly with his thumb. He was driving me wild, and we hadn't gotten to the main event yet. He put his tongue inside of me, and I bucked hard against his face. He pinned my hips to the couch more forcefully, and he began tongue fucking me in earnest. With each lick, I felt myself go higher.

Alonso was tired of foreplay. "Let's go to the bedroom." He slid his arms under me, and he carried me to a bedroom. Like the living room, this room was also gold themed.

I barely had time to notice that, though, because Alonso was taking off his clothes. His dick was massive. He had the build of a swimmer, with broad shoulders and tight abs.

"It's so sexy when you look at me like that, love."

Victor was taking off his clothes, too. They were identical in almost every way, except Alonso had a spiraling dragon tattooed on his left hip.

"Cool tattoo," I said, as the two of them advanced towards me on the bed.

"You like dragons?"

"I love dragons. I used to dream about becoming one. Dragons are so powerful and wealthy. I guess that's just in stories, though." It was a strange conversation to be having when naked, but they had a way of making me open up.

"Well, this dragon wants to fuck you now." Alonso pushed me on my back, put a pillow under my hips, and pulled my legs over his shoulders. He bumped my dripping hole with the head of his cock.

"Mate me."

"Yes. Please. Please."

He pushed it into me. It hurt for a second, then it felt amazing. He thrust and retreated, and it felt better than anything ever had.

Victor wasn't going to miss out on the fun. He went to the top of the bed, and he straddled my face while putting his hands on the wall above me.

"Suck me."

I'd never done this before, but I was willing to try. From the way that he moaned when I licked my way around the crown of his dick, he liked it. He began to thrust rhythmically into my mouth in counterpoint with Alonso's thrusts inside of me. I could taste his precum, and it was delicious and salty. I could feel the muscles in his thighs tense, and I knew he was about to come. In the second before he shot into my mouth, he pulled out.

"No. This first time, it is inside of you. Alonso, pull out."

Alonso growled, but he pulled out. Victor laid on his back. His hand was on his dick, and his hard cock was pointing straight up.

"Mate me."

I straddled his body, and I took his cock slowly into me. I was so wet that it slid in with no resistance. I hesitated when I had all of him inside of me, to get used to the sensations at this angle.

"Kiss me." I leaned down to kiss him. He put his tongue in my mouth, and we fought for dominance of the kiss.

Alonso came up behind me, and he pushed me so that my entire torso was flat on Victor's. He started gathering wetness from my thighs and pushing it past my taint to my asshole. I tensed up and stopped kissing Victor. I put my hands and was about to push up.

"Shh," he soothed. "I won't hurt you."

I relaxed, and I settled back into making out with Victor. He was a much gentler kisser than Alonso. Victor was, in so many ways, more of a gentleman than Alonso. Alonso took what he wanted. Victor did, too, but I knew he'd always ask for something new if he could.

Alonso pushed his thumb inside of my ass. It was covered in my juices, but my sphincter was tight. Nothing had ever been up there before. He pushed just a little in and out, getting deeper with each thrust from Victor.

The scent of sex was in the air. The rhythm with Victor got harder and faster, and I stopped Frenching him in order not to bite his tongue with the intensity of my impending orgasm. Victor put his big hands on my hips, and he pulled me hard into him, getting even deeper. I cried out as I came, ecstasy bursting inside of me. I panted hard. I rested on Victor's chest, limp with the force of my orgasm.

Both of them were still hard.

"Do you trust me?" Alonso's accent was so sexy.

"Yeah."

He pulled apart my ass cheeks, and he pushed something that was way bigger than his thumb towards my ass.

"Relax. It'll be better. I just have to get past the beginning."

Victor wasn't thrusting now. He was stationary. Slowly, Alonso pushed his dick, still lubricated with my juices, inside of my ass. It burned, yes, but it felt incredible. With two cocks inside of me, I felt like I should be bursting. However, it was perfect. They were perfect.

Alonso pulled back, and he thrust into me again. I threw my head back and gasped for breath. He took a handful of my hair, and he kept me arched like that.

"I like the way you feel." My glutes were pressed on him. He roughly pushed into me. Victor set up the rhythm again, too. They coordinated pushing into me. Each would retreat when the other advanced. I was helpless, stuck between them, sweat on all of our skin.

Alonso picked up the pace, and Victor responded accordingly. I put my face into Victor's neck, and he swept a soothing hand down my back. Alonso slapped my ass hard.

"I'm so close."

Alonso pulled my hair even harder as I felt the first of his hot seed spill into my ass. I fluttered around him in my own orgasm. With a grunt, Victor began to release, too, inside of my womb.

Alonso rolled off of me. In the aftermath, this didn't seem like Vegas.

"I'm not on the pill."

"We didn't think you were."

"You didn't use condoms."

"We're clean, and you're a virgin."

"I was a virgin. But I'm not worried about sexually transmitted diseases. What if I get pregnant?"

"If you get pregnant, it would be a tremendous gift." Victor was so serious, even though we were naked in bed. All of us were covered in various amounts of bodily fluids.

"I have a life, you know. Getting pregnant would really ruin going to college and holding down a job. I can barely afford to provide for myself, let alone a baby."

"Money's not a problem for us. We'd support you in whatever you chose to do. We could buy a college for you."

I snorted. "Be real." I looked into his eyes.

Victor looked dead serious. "I am."

I got off of him. My pussy and ass felt so empty compared to before. "You're being weird." I looked around for my clothes, then I remembered that my clothes hadn't made it into the bedroom.

I looked down at myself and sighed. I didn't want to get jizz and blood all over my clothes. I didn't have that many in Ecuador, so I needed to clean up. I went to their bathroom.

I ran the sink, but Alonso's hand went to turn the faucet off.

"Hey!"

"Shower." He picked me up and put me in the shower. They had cross jets at shoulder height that sprayed my body with water. Both of them were fully erect again. Victor and Alonso got in with me. Victor's back was against the wall, and Alonso was at my front. Alonso pulled me into his arms, and my legs were around him. He pushed into me. Even though I felt sore, it felt so good that I didn't protest as he set up a rhythm.

Victor kissed the center of the back of my neck, and he snaked his hand around to play with my clit as his brother thrust into me. He took his other hand to part my ass cheeks. I was still plenty wet inside, and he shoved into me, without the waiting that Alonso had done. It burned, but I knew how good it would feel once he got all the way in.

The spray of the water was all around us. Alonso was pushing me harder and harder into Victor. I could feel their dicks swelling inside of me, and they burst, shooting seed into me.

In the aftermath, Alonso set me on my feet. He kissed the top of my head. "Thank you."

Victor was soaping up his hands. "Come here." He lathered the soap on my back, on my neck, on my breasts. His hand went down the center of my body, and he slid his slick, soapy hand into me.

"We need to clean you up." He pulled it from my clit to my back door. He kissed my shoulder.

"Close your eyes." Alonso was pouring shampoo on his hand, and he started to wash my hair. It felt so good and intimate. He captured my mouth again. This time, it wasn't foreplay. It was just kissing, with the three of us in the shower.

When they had cleaned every inch of my body, they turned off the water jets. Alonso picked me up again to set carefully on their marble bathroom countertop. He took a towel, and he dried me off, paying special attention to my breasts, which still bore the marks of being bitten by him. He was completely unconcerned with his own nudity, and his body was a masterpiece, especially with the dragon tattoo on his hip. He saw me looking at it.

"Would you like to be a dragon? It just takes a bite."

I didn't know what he was playing at, but it felt good when he bit me.

"Yes."

Victor came to my other side. Both of them bent down to bite my shoulders, and I felt my body get aroused again, even after all my orgasms. It shot pain and pleasure inside of me, racing neck and neck for dominance. They bit hard enough to just barely break the skin, and I could feel their tongues soothe the places their teeth had pierced.

"Come, let's get you clothes." Victor wrapped a towel around me, and he picked me up to carry to the bedroom. "Do you like blue or black?"

"Blue, I guess." Victor shifted so my weight was on one hand. It was still effortless for him. He reached for a blue robe inside of the closet. He carried me to the bed, and he let me sit down.

"Here." He helped me put the robe on. I tied the sash. I could see myself in the closet mirror, though, and I still had bite marks on my cleavage from Alonso.

"There's something we need to talk about."

MIRROR, MIRROR

I laid back, feeling content. "Yeah, what's that?" I put my hands behind my head and crossed my legs.

"You're a dragon now."

That got my attention in a hurry. I sat up. "What?"

"You consented to being Changed."

"I did no such thing."

"You agreed to mate us, and you agreed to becoming a dragon."

This guy was clearly unbalanced. "Okay…" I needed to bolt so I could get my clothes.

Victor put his hand on my arm. "No, look." His arm changed so that it was covered in purple scales.

I started to hyperventilate. Alonso closed the bedroom door. "Stay and hear us out."

I didn't really have a choice. "Ok." The second I could manage it, I was bolting out of this madhouse.

"You're our mate for life. We'll cherish you with every breath we take." Victor used such pretty words.

"We'll mate every day." Alonso sometimes did not.

Victor watched me carefully. "You know how I asked about your last name?"

"Yes."

"It was to check that our first instinct was correct. We knew it from the moment that we saw you that you could be our mate."

"How?"

"Your smell and your abundant curves." Alonso trailed a hand from my boobs to my ass.

"Not very many women could become a dragon. For a lot of them, their body would reject the Change. For you, though, drinking our blood did not make you immediately throw up."

"I did *not* drink your blood."

"You did, though. It was in the beer."

"How could you slip it in my beer without asking me first?"

"We did. We asked you if you would mate us if we could make you happy, and you said yes. You are ours for eternity."

"You'll never have to worry about money again. We have long lifespans."

"What about my real life? It's not like I can hide out in the Andes forever. People will notice that I'm gone."

"That's easy." Victor flicked his fingers, and a perfect copy of me appeared. "We'll send a simulacrum in your place."

"People will be able to tell it's not me."

"No one will be able to tell it's not you. You haven't noticed the simulacrum in your group."

"What? Who?" Please let it be Catie.

"It's the one you call Alice. She mated two dragons in the Galapagos recently."

I gaped at them. "What? No. She's my best friend. I would know."

"The simulacrum was made by someone right by her. She's the queen of the Brood, too, so that doesn't hurt. The magic is very strong. All simulacra are formulated to act exactly as the human would act."

"Alice is a dragon queen?" This talk was so bizarre.

"Yes. Would you like to speak with her? We can form a telepathic link using any mirror." Victor raised his hand and said a few short, emphatic words. The mirror on the closet showed me Alice.

I walked up to it. "Hello?"

She looked up. "Oh my gosh! Gab!" She pressed her hands on her side of the mirror. "Gab! I wish I could hug you right now."

"What are you doing in the mirror?"

"You know, don't you? Victor and Alonso called in for permission earlier today to find a mate. I got interested when they told me her name was Gabriella."

I felt tears prick my eyes. "How could you leave me and never say a word?"

"I couldn't. But my simulacrum was there to keep you company."

"It's not the same as you."

"It is, though. It's the life that I would've lived if I hadn't chosen to be queen. I see everything that happens to my simulacrum in dreams. It's hard to differentiate between dreams and reality. I don't know if I'm living a normal life and dreaming about being a queen, or living as a queen and dreaming about real life. Maybe this is all happening as we both dream from our beds in our apartments."

"I can assure you that I am awake."

She smiled. "You would say that. Anyway, do you want to join the Brood?"

"The Brood?"

"It's our extended family. The purple dragons have South America, and I lead them."

"If you're real, then I think I'm already a dragon."

"Try. Try to change your hand into a claw."

I looked down at my hands. Neither of them turned into a claw.

"I don't think I'm a dragon."

Alice rolled her eyes. "You aren't really trying. Imagine that your hand is a claw. What shape is it? It's purple with scales. You have talons."

I looked down and imagined my hand as she described it. My hand changed.

"Holy shit!"

"You'll get used to it, I promise."

"Don't you miss me? Don't you miss our real life? Is being a dragon queen totally normal to you now?"

Alice sighed. "Yes, I've settled into being a dragon queen. Of course I miss you. I've missed you every day that I've been here. But I can't go back. My simulacrum is living my life. I have another one here now, doing important things for a lot of people. That's what you want most, isn't it?"

First, happiness. Now, impact. But both answers were true. "Yes."

"You can be the Viceroy of the Andes, if you want."

"You can do that?"

"I'm the queen. I can do anything." She smiled like a cat who got the cream. "You can make an impact. You can help thousands upon thousands of dragons. And once you learn to fly, you can go anywhere in the world that you want to be."

It sounded pretty tempting. "I don't know if I want to live a double life like you, though. It sounds really disorienting to bounce between two realities."

"You could always let your simulacrum disappear, you know. You'd just have to 'die' in a plausible way, that's all."

Alonso cut in on our girl talk. "We could do it on a zipline."

Alice nodded, encouraging him to continue with her hand. "Go on."

"It's simple. Her carabiner fails, and she falls into the cloud forest. No one will ever be able to find her body. There won't even be one. We'll just take back the magic in the simulacrum."

"How does that sound?" Alice turned to me. I was clad in a robe, and I felt self-conscious.

"Will you guys really make sure that I'm happy for every day of the rest of my life?" I needed to feel sure of that before I could make the decision to leave my old life behind.

"We promise." They both had their hands over their hearts.

"Dragon oaths are sacred. If they ever break their promises, their blood will boil in their veins. There is no cure."

I nodded. "Ok. I'm in."

"You guys need to get busy then. I'll talk to you soon, Gab." Alice waved goodbye, and the mirror went back to being a mirror.

"What do we need to do?"

"First, we need to take the pin out of a carabiner so that it looks like it's whole but isn't. I think that we need to do this on the first line, because the carabiner won't hold for long."

"Ok."

"I can take you first in front of your friends, and you'll be on your own when you drop."

"Why do you guys even work anyway, if you have so much money and can actually fly?"

"I like interacting with people. Mindo is a quiet place. There's not much variety here."

"Why do you live here at all, then?"

"Can you keep a secret?"

"Yes, of course."

"This is where some of the Incan gold is."

"You mean the Incan gold that Atahualpa told his people not to send to the conquistadors?"

"Yes, that Incan gold."

Shit. I guessed that explained the decor of their home.

"Can't you move it?"

"It's in the mountain."

"Can't you take it out?"

"You don't understand. It's *in* the mountain. It can't be taken out without unstablizing the mountain."

"Oh. Ok."

"We should send you back. Your friends will worry if you are gone all night. I'll walk you back to Casa de Celia."

Victor walked me back to the main room, and I picked up my clothes and got dressed. He pulled me into him with an arm around my shoulders in the cold night, and I huddled into his body heat. He felt like a furnace, which was wonderful in the Andes at night.

It took a few minutes to get to the hostel. We were quiet on the way over, each thinking our own thoughts. Outside of the hostel, he bent to kiss me. "Until tomorrow."

"Tomorrow," I promised.

ZIPLINE

lice's simulacrum was waiting up for me when I got back. "How was it? Was it great?"

"It was great." I could never look at this simulacrum the same again. "I need to rest now." It was past midnight, and we were going to the ecological station in the morning before dawn.

Bright and early, my cell phone alarm went off. I made Alice's simulacrum get out of bed, and I brushed my teeth.

A truck came to get us, and it took us to the ecological reserve. A German ecologist came out to greet us.

She walked us through the forest, identifying all the plants by name.

"Do you notice that every flower is some shade of red or pink?"

We looked around. Everything looked like it belonged in the room of a 5-year-old princess. "Yeah."

"That's because hummingbirds, which are major pollinators in the cloud forest, can see infrared. The more red you are, the greater chance you have of reproduction. There are thousands of hummingbirds. We've recorded more than 200 species just on sight."

We walked through the cloud forest as she explained everything to us, and we ended up back at the reserve at the end of the trail, which looped.

"I will give you hierba luisa tea. I think you will find it good." She lead us to a porch. In front of the porch was a bunch of birdfeeders. There were dozens of hummingbirds there, and none of them were alike. She poured all of us a hot cup of tea, and we sat and watched the hummingbirds flit around crazily, eating a bit here and there.

When all of us had finished our tea, she took us back to where we'd met the truck. It was idling there, and it took us back to Casa de Celia.

When we got back to Casa de Celia, Victor was waiting in a truck. This was it. This was the last I'd see of my old life. I had packed everything into my backpack the night before. Alonso would make sure that it ended up in their home. They were sending someone to my home in Quito to gather my belongings before the news of my "death" hit my host parents. I knew my mom wouldn't care if my stuff went missing, but my host parents probably would notice if I died and suddenly all of my stuff disappeared after the funeral.

The guy in the passenger seat was no one I'd seen before. All of us girls climbed in the back, and we took the short ride to the ziplining place. The new guy, who introduced himself as Jorge, lead the front, while Victor hung back with me.

"I'm going to make you invisible and send your simulacrum now. Don't panic. I'll teach you how to do it yourself later."

I nodded. He said a few words. I looked down at myself. I waved my hand in front of my face. I couldn't see it.

"You can still make noise, so you need to be careful. I just thought you'd like to see this yourself."

"Ok."

Victor hurried to catch up with the others, and my simulacrum hurried, too. He outfitted her with all the gear and the faulty carabiner. He pushed his way to the front of the line, and he set her up on the line. I held my breath as she zoomed out to the middle, and she screamed as she fell down. Fitz, Catie, and Jade were screaming too. Alice simulacrum's face was shocked. Jorge sat down hard on the ground.

"Mierda."

Gabriella Peres was gone.

EPILOGUE

After I faked my death, all of my stuff was put in Victor and Alonso's house. Alice made me the Viceroy of the Andes, and my life settled into a comfortable rhythm of governing the Andean region.

I was sad that I'd missed out on all the trips to the Amazon and the tropical coast that my group would take, but my new life was worth every bit of the sacrifice I'd made.

PUYO

Book Three • Puyo

Chased
by the
Dragons

PARANORMAL SHIFTER ROMANCE

ALYSE ZAFTIG

WITH

EVA WILDER

CHOCOLATE CAKE

I was so tired from wading through my ecology of Ecuador class. It was really interesting to me, but I was definitely behind all the other kids. They all were majoring in Biology of Environmental Science, and they'd had all this material before. As a Spanish major, I'd never heard of keystone species or been exposed to how important ocean currents were. Add to that the difficulty of taking upper-level ecology classes in Spanish, and you've got a recipe for some late nights cuddling with a Spanish dictionary alongside Wikipedia in English.

When I finally finished, far after the rest of the group, I went into the computer lab, which was where we hung out. Catie, Fitz, and Alice were in there, sharing chocolate cake from the bakery next to our building. They had a conversation class right before my ecology class. I ate chocolate at home; it seems like almost everyone did. However, in Ecuador, the chocolate was on another level. It was grown here, and some of the freshest chocolate I'd ever had was here. I'd had Swiss chocolate in Switzerland, French chocolate in France, and Belgian chocolate in Belgium from the royal confectioner. They were great, but Ecuadorian chocolate tasted different to me, somehow. European chocolate felt smooth, while Ecuadorian chocolate was more earthy for its mouth-feel.

Catie covered her mouth. "Do you want some, Jade?" she offered politely. I could tell from the body language of Fitz and Alice that they weren't inclined to share, though. They were bringing their cake a little closer to them.

"No, I'm good. Thanks for the offer, though."

Catie nodded, took a sip of her tea, and went back to eating her cake.

I sat down at the table and sighed. "That was so hard, guys. Maybe not for everyone else, but for me it's so hard."

Catie made a sympathetic noise. "I know you're trying the best you can."

"I've never had problems in school, you know? It's always been so easy, but I swear this is going from zero to sixty in less than a month. The professor expects us to already be familiar with the concepts, and he just glosses over them like it's nothing. He's Chilean, too, so he uses different words, and he writes all over the board in an incoherent way. He also says 'chuta' so much that we've started betting batidos before class on who can guess the number of times he says it."

Alice laughed. "That's the funniest thing I've heard in my life."

I rolled my eyes. "It would be funny if it weren't so annoying, I guess. Anyways, what are you guys up to?"

"We're planning a trip to Baños and Puyo starting tomorrow. We were planning on taking a tour from a company that starts in Baños, which will take us in a private car to Puyo, and then getting a bus back to Quito from there. Are you in?"

For a month, we hadn't ventured outside of Quito. Gabriella's death in the cloud forest had shaken us all. There wasn't even a body to send back to the United States, since she'd dropped into the middle of the cloud forest. What was really weird was that all her stuff had disappeared from her host parents' apartment before they were notified of her death. If there had been a burglar, then the burglar had been surprisingly picky to only take stuff out of one room — even the worthless stuff like her shampoo — and leave the Xbox, TV, and other expensive electronics that her host parents had. They had filed a report, but the police force wasn't too interested in recovering the mostly worthless belongings of a dead girl. If the American embassy got involved, it could have pushed them into action. However, nobody higher up really believed that it was important enough to get involved in.

Once, our literature professor told us about a friend of his who owned an Internet cafe. Everyone brought in a backpack and set it at his or her feet while he or she browsed the web. They had someone run in and grab a backpack. They'd quickly apprehended him, and they had security camera footage to show it. They'd taken him to the police station, only to be turned away by the police. The police didn't think it was worth anything. The percentage of unsolved murders in Ecuador was around 80%.

We'd held a small memorial service for her, with all of us. It was like our monthly birthday gatherings with the whole program, but much sadder. We'd all bought flower wreaths. Alice had given a eulogy, and she'd cried during it. None of us felt much like traveling, and we wouldn't go back to Mindo in a hurry after watching our friend die in the endless orchid canopy of the cloud forest. There didn't seem to be any legal liability for having unsafe lines. The twin guides had disappeared, and the Ecuadorian justice system seemingly had no interest in ensuring public safety for zipliners.

We only had a semester here, though, so we needed to make the most of it. We'd already been to Baños, but we'd never been to Puyo.

"I'm in."

"Cool."

"What time are we leaving?"

"We were planning on meeting at Quitumbe around 8 AM. Just text all of us when you get there."

"Can do." I got up. "My host mom is expecting me to come home early today, because she's going to leave town to visit her son in Guayaquil. I gotta go."

"Bye," everyone chorused.

I put on my backpack, and I headed home.

QUITUMBE

The next morning, bright and early, I took the Ecovia down to the bus that would take me to Quitumbe in time to meet the others. I was yawning like crazy, but it was fine. I swore that next time I'd just take a taxi; it was cheap, and it was faster. There were zillions of taxis in Quito.

Alice, Fitz, and Catie were there. Catie was such a chipper person, and she looked like there was no place she'd rather be. Fitz and Alice looked like they'd like to take an eight-hour nap. Maybe 10.

"We bought our boletos," Catie told me. "Here's your ticket." She handed the ticket to me.

"Oh, you didn't have to. That's so thoughtful of you! How much was it?"

"It was five bucks."

I dug around in my backpack. "Here. Thanks for going to the trouble of getting a ticket for me." She was such a sweetheart.

Catie waved me aside. "Don't worry about paying me back. You can spot me at dinner or buy me some batidos. It's all good." She smiled at me.

"Thanks, sweetie." I put the money back in my backpack. It always came out in the wash. "Let's go grab the bus." I turned sharply.

I set a brisk pace, and Catie went with me. Alice and Fitz shambled slowly behind us. All of us put our stuff into the bus, and then we handed our boletos to the bus driver. A lot of Ecuadorians simply gave money directly to the driver, but when the bus was full, the people who held ticket stubs were allowed to sit. The other often stood in the aisles. It wasn't that safe, honestly, but it worked.

One time, in Cuenca, we'd taken a bus back from Ingapirca. There was a perfectly round lady with chickens inside of a cage and a green shawl made of llama wool. It was raining outside, so the shawl was wet. The strong llama smell was awful. The American legal recruiter we'd added to our entourage at the hostel was a gentleman, and he gave his seat to the llama lady when he saw her lurching around the aisle with every jolt of the bus, chickens squawking in their cage. Instead of sitting on her seat, like a normal person, she'd taken the opportunity to sit in my lap, shoving the llama smell as close to me as she could get and somehow managing to resist my attempts to push her off of me. I tried to convince her to get off, to no avail. She did not speak Spanish, and she only spoke kichwa. The chickens were salt in the wound. I prayed to any deity that would hear me that I would not have a llama lady sitting in my lap on this trip.

When we got in the bus, I sat next to Alice. Fitz and Catie were in the seat behind us. Alice closed her eyes to go to sleep, before the bus even moved. Fitz was not far behind. I closed my eyes and drifted off.

AMAZON RAIN FOREST

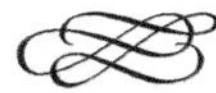

When I woke up, we were already in Baños. Catie was poking Fitz, and I gently touched Alice's shoulder.

"Hey. Get up. It's time to go."

She opened one eye, then the other. "What?"

"We're in Baños. We've got to grab our stuff, and then we can head to the tour place so we can tell them to expect us tomorrow morning."

Alice yawned. "Ok."

We headed out, put on our backpacks, and then headed to the office. We booked a tour for the four of us to go to Puyo and stay at an ecolodge in the Amazon. The itinerary was pretty fast. We started at the meeting point in Baños, then we'd hit a rescue center for animals, including ocelots and caimans. We'd have lunch at the lodge. Then, we'd go to a waterfall where we could swim. They'd take us on a night hike to see the nocturnal animals after dark. The next day, we'd go to visit an indigenous community in the jungle, where we'd watch them make traditional clay pots. We'd be able to shoot darts with the blowpipe and paint our faces with red achiote. We'd canoe on the Puyo river, grab lunch, and then head back. It was going to be a really full trip.

Before that, though, we could walk around Baños for the rest of today. We needed to find a hostel for tonight, and then we'd eat some lunch. They had puenting, which was bridge jumping, here and I wanted to try it out. Last time, we'd gone whitewater rafting and horseback riding on Tungurahua, which was an active volcano that sometimes spewed ash. It was incredibly cool to ride around on an active volcano, but it wasn't an experience that I needed to repeat. It also was pretty expensive for Ecuador.

"Hey, guys. Do you want to get settled, eat lunch, and then go puenting?"

"No," Fitz said. "There's no way that I'd go puenting on a full stomach."

She had a point. "How about we set our stuff down, then we go puenting, and then we eat lunch?"

Everyone nodded. We went to a hostel called Hostel Maria, and we got a room with two queen beds for the four of us. I asked the hostel proprietor where the puenting office was, and he pointed us in the right direction. It was only a block away.

They did puenting trips on the hour every hour. We put on harnesses, and we waited on a bench outside for a blue bus to arrive. When it did, it took us straight to a bridge that went over a whitewater river. It was terrifying. I watched the people on the bridge cling to the side. The puenting instructors straight up just pushed people off the platform. I already knew that I was acrophobic; I have a significant terror of heights. I felt like it was a bad idea, but I already had my gear on, and everyone else was jumping off the bridge.

"Who wants to go first?"

"Me," Fitz said. She was the most fearless out of all of us, the adventurer who'd spent last semester in Hungary and traveled to 15 countries during that semester.

"Jump, and lean forward," the instructor told Fitz.

She nodded. She got hooked up to the puenting ropes, and she went over the side. When she looked over the edge, she choked. "Holy shit, no. I'm not going over." The puenting instructor tried to push her off, but Fitz was an athlete. She was stronger than the puenting instructor, especially when she definitely did not want to move an inch and she had a solid bridge to cling to.

"I'll go." I got hooked up to the ropes while Fitz fought the pushes of her instructor. I looked over at her, then I looked down at the white water of the river below. I leapt off of the platform.

FALLING

I spread out like a flying squirrel or a skydiver. As the instructor told me, I leaned forward. I felt the air rush past me, and I was freefalling down. My body thought that I was dying, but it gave me clarity of thought. There was only me, the rope, and the river. I flipped completely over, and I felt my neck snap back as the rope pulled me taut at the end. I swung back and forth like a pendulum, which was why another word for puenting was pendulo. There was an instructor with a red jacket down below who pulled me to the side using the ropes, at a little platform. I was standing on firm ground again.

As the instructor pulled off all of my gear, I could feel how wobbly my knees were. I hadn't just done another extreme sport, which I did all the time in Ecuador. I'd literally jumped off of a bridge, despite my acrophobia. My body was full of happy endorphins, even though I still wasn't very steady on my feet.

I heard a scream. She had lost the battle to stay on the platform. Fitz was coming in now, and she dangled back and forth. When she stopped swinging so much, the red-jacketed instructor pulled her down, too. When she got close, I saw that she was crying. Her mascara, the only makeup she wore because of her light lashes, was running.

I took baby steps over to her, and I hugged her.

"Hey. Hey. It's ok. You're just fine."

She clung to me briefly, and then she stepped back.

"My legs are so shaky. Holy shit, that was scary."

"I'm proud of you for doing this." I patted her back. "Why don't we go up top to meet the others? We can video them as they come down."

"Good idea."

Fitz, the marathon runner who ran with Lauren, slowly made her way up the hill. I was right behind her, willing to give her a boost. My legs were steadier, too, because I'd had a minute more to adjust. They still felt like noodles, though.

When we got to the lookout point, I whipped out my camera and took videos of Catie and Alice going over. Catie screamed, "Holy shit!" as she fell over the side. Alice went over without much fanfare, as if she jumped off of bridges every day of her life. In some things, she was such a cool customer. They both got pulled to the side.

Catie sat down. She was shaking so hard that it was visible from our vantage point. Alice was more sanguine. She was smiling a little. She waved at Fitz and me, and she began to go up the hill.

"That was so much fun."

Catie snorted, and she slowly followed Alice up. "If your definition of fun is going into a death defying dive while hooked to a rope that will give you mad whiplash, yeah."

That was the feistiest I ever heard Catie get. "Girl, loosen up. It's fun. I'd never do that in the United States."

"It's prohibitively expensive in the United States." She rubbed the back of her neck. "For a good reason, too. Can you imagine the cost of the insurance for people who enable bungee jumping?"

Catie was such a buzzkill sometimes.

"Whatever." I gathered up everything we'd brought with us. "Who's up for dinner?"

Everyone was.

DUSSELDORF

They drove us back into town, and we went back to our hostel. We stowed our cameras and other gear away, and we picked up our purses. They were always heavy. In the US, I was used to using my debit or credit cards; in Ecuador, everything was in efectivo, that cash money. Ecuador was the only place that actually used Sacagawea coins, which were far more durable than flimsy dollar bills. Coins last 30 years, while dollar bills have a lifespan a small fraction of that. I got Sacagawea coins for change everywhere, since I was a baller American paying in twenties. Every cashier held up my $20 bill to the light, to make sure that it was real. In a country where most people lived on $2 a day or less, $20 meant a lot. In Otovalo, I bought gorgeous multicolored handmade scarves for $1 or $2 a piece, and both of us considered the transaction a bargain. The only place that would accept $100 bills was the MegaMaxi near our school.

Instead of carrying just a wallet, I had to carry a purse, which was a pain. In the Ecovia, Lauren had had her purse slit. She'd only noticed when she got off. They hadn't gotten much, just her wallet with her RFID to get into our school, but it was annoying that theft was so prevalent. Ecuador was a beautiful country full of warm people, but it also was not what I would consider excessively safe.

As a result, all of us were careful, more than we would be somewhere back home. I was mostly immune from thieves. As an Asian, I blended better than my blonde American friends or Fitz, who was our only ginger. Because Ecuador and China allowed their citizens to move freely between the two countries, there were a lot of Chinese people in Ecuador.

I'm not Chinese at all, but everyone calls me Chinita here. At a party at a friend's house, I had a conversation with this guy who played World of Warcraft with a lot of Americans, which was how he brushed up on his conversational English. When he got excited, he started swearing in Spanish. He got a lot of heat for it, and they kept telling him, "Mexican, go home. You don't belong here." First, he was physically located in Ecuador. And second, he wasn't Mexican. It made him really upset to be called Mexican when he was clearly from another country.

I'd empathized with that.

"I get that a lot, too. I'm Vietnamese, but they call me Chinita all the time."

He laughed. "Oh, but I do that. You're Chinese."

"I'm not, though. I'm from a different country. Well, my parents were. I've never been there."

"Oh, no, it's the same thing. Chinese and Vietnamese. They are the same."

I'd left it there, but I'd never hung out with that guy again. I may be technically mixed race because of the tiny smidgen of French, Basque to be exact, blood in my family, the smidgen that gave me a Basque last name, but I definitely was not Chinese at all.

We walked around downtown, and we looked for places to eat. Not surprisingly, most of the restaurants in town featured Ecuadorian food. Even Ecuadorian Asian fusion food, chifa, didn't sound good to me. After so many months of eating Ecuadorian food at home, we were long past the point where we wanted to eat it for every meal. I had started eating Chicken McNuggets at the McDonald's in Quicentro once a week. I didn't even eat McDonald's in the United States. However, there was something about eating foreign food day in and day out that made me want to eat some American comfort food.

We settled into a restaurant named Dusseldorf. It was run by a nice German man who could feed us bratwurst. There was an incredible German presence in Ecuador, *and* the nice German man accepted credit cards. Eating dinner wouldn't cost any Sacagawea coins. He took our order, and we actually got the food that we ordered about 15 minutes later. Ecuadorian service is not like that.

Catie was not in the mood to hang around for dessert or walk around town, so I walked her home. Alice and Fitz walked around Baños that night. The town was small, and we had our cell phones.

Mobile phones had been one of the first things we had purchased when we had arrived in Ecuador. Cell phones were simultaneously more expensive and cheaper than the United States. Ecuadorians did not subsidize cell phone costs, like Americans did. You had to pay the full price of a cell phone in cash. Because Ecuador exacted a 100% tariff on any technology that came into the country, you ended up paying 200% of the retail price of any phone.

I could have bought a Blackberry for an exorbitant amount, but I, an impecunious youth like my peers, bought a tiny red-and-black basic cell phone from Movistar. They didn't have cell phone plans that locked you in for two years in Ecuador. Instead, they had pay as you go. If you topped up your balance on certain days, you'd get 3x the amount that you'd paid. There was a minimum of $6 to get that. However, $6 to get $18 of phone credit seemed cheap to me.

While that was an incredible deal for all of the Americans, that was far beyond the pocket of most Ecuadorians. Life is astoundingly cheaper the wealthier you are; the more money you have, the more often you can buy in bulk. In-network calls were cheaper than out-of-network calls, and almost all of us had the same cell phone plans as our host parents, who took us to the stores as part of our orientation. Host parents like mine, who were too busy to do something as banal as take me into Quicentro when I arrived, went with someone from the study abroad program the weekend after that to pick up our phones. When I realized that the cheapest phone there would cost $88 in cash, I was glad that I was carrying a $100 bill. They had taken a photocopy of the $100 bill; outside of MegaMaxi, that was pretty common.

The nice thing about having a cell phone coupled with Google Voice was that I could text home for only the cost that my service provider exacted. I didn't have to pay international rates to stay in touch. It was like I was there but out of sight. I uploaded my pictures and videos to Facebook, and it was as if they were looking over my shoulder anyway.

My best friend was spending the semester in Costa Rica. She was a biology major who was living on Cocos Island. Both of us wrote at least one Facebook message to each other a day, and often we'd done more than that. We had more than 1,000 messages from this semester, and that didn't include the emails that we sent each other. We always had each other's back, and we'd been proofreading our essays for our classes. The number of Facebook messages would be more if I'd been able to afford a smartphone or really been willing to pay for it. It seemed stupid, though, to spend hundreds of dollars on a cell phone that would only work in Ecuador. It would be locked on Movistar. So, I'd done the financially prudent thing and had a brick cell phone that looked like the ones my parents had when I was really young.

I actually used T9, both in English and Spanish. It was honestly faster than typing with my thumbs on my iPhone's keyboard back home. The throwback phone was really easy to use. Fitz called me out on it once, because I had the fastest thumbs in the West.

"Do you stand by your cell phone waiting forever?"

I looked at her. "No."

"You always answer texts so fast. Sometimes you reply before my phone even confirms that the text was sent."

I shrugged. That was her phone's problem, not mine.

I spoke Spanish almost as well as Alice. I had a lot of Hispanic friends back home. When I had a heavy tan, I could pass as a Hispanic girl. There is a lot of stigma associated with dark skin in Vietnamese culture, and I was called African-American by my aunts. I shrugged it off. American culture prizes dark skin and calls pale people pasty. Vietnamese culture prizes pale skin and calls dark-skinned people black. One of my cousins was pretty dark-skinned, and his family nickname was "Blackie."

I didn't call him that. I just called him Robbie, which he preferred and every American called him, anyway. Americans have a strange relationship with race. It was much easier for them to call him Robbie than Tuan, his Vietnamese name. I personally didn't feel like Tuan was very hard to pronounce, since it rhymes with one, but a lot of people had given Robbie grief about it over the years. Almost nobody called him Tuan, because it just wasn't worth the hassle for him to correct someone else.

SPEED AND EUCHRE

hen we got back to the hostel, Catie got out a pack of cards. She was still pretty freaked out and unusually quiet. She was pale. She dealt the cards so that we could play Speed.

"Are you ok?" Catie's bubbly personality was an essential part of her. I didn't know how to act around her when she wasn't being the ultra-supportive cheerleader.

She caught my eyes. "I just haven't done anything like that before, you know? And I feel like you guys had a much easier time dealing with it than I did."

"That's not true at all. I think that you were brave to try something new. I'm acrophobic, and I think that you've done incredibly well, considering that we kinda went puenting out of the blue."

"It was Fitz who wanted it." Catie crossed her arms tightly. "I really wish we hadn't gone."

"Catie," I said. "It was a once-in-a-lifetime experience. I'm not running back to that bridge so I can watch the river come towards me again, but you did something that scared you. I did something that scared me. We got out of our comfort zones. That's a central component of studying abroad. Remember how we talked about cognitive dissonance and the Stroop test when we first arrived."

Catie nodded, and she loosened her arms. "I remember."

"I know that it seems really foreign. Quite a few things seem foreign here, but you are having all kinds of adventures, and I think that you're going to have so many stories to tell when you get home."

Catie rubbed her face with her hands. "I guess."

"Let's play Speed, hm?"

Catie nodded.

"Three, two, one." I counted down right before we flipped the cards over so that we could start at the same time. Speed was played in a lot of different ways, and all of us played slightly differently. Catie's version included slapping sandwiches and doubles. When you slapped, the other person was required to pick up the bigger pile and put it in their hand. It was a long game because you continued to replenish your draw pile.

It kept us occupied until Alice and Fitz finally wandered in, holding a six-pack of Coke. Alice put the six-pack on the ground, and she lay face-down on her bed.

"Hey, guys." Fitz sat on the bed that Catie and I were sharing tonight. "Do you want to play something?"

"I'd love to." I looked at Catie. "Are you ok with switching from Speed?"

"We could play three-way Speed," Catie offered.

Fitz shrugged. "I'd rather play Euchre."

"Euchre sounds good to me." I had needed to coddle Catie a little bit more right after we jumped off the bridge, but she didn't need me to hold her hand all the time. The other girls in the group would be surprised to know this, but Catie had a pretty solid steel backbone under all the bubbliness. I was the one closest to Catie, and I knew that she had a lot more serious thoughts under being the ditz of our group. I loved her, in her own way, even though she talked too much sometimes. But that trait helped me. As long as I stayed in her shadow, I didn't have to talk very much.

Catie sighed. "Euchre it is." She collected all of my cards, and she started shuffling the deck together.

"Alice, come on." I turned to her bed, where she was still prostrate. "Don't you want to play Euchre?"

"Fine." She pushed herself up, and she went to stand by my bed. "Who is partnering with whom?"

"I'll partner with Catie. You and Fitz can go together." I moved so that she'd fit with us.

"Who wants to deal first?" Catie offered the deck to everyone.

"You can go first." It saved time. In euchre, being the dealer was both a blessing and a curse. It was like a mini-leadership position. On the plus side, you could get the plum benefits of picking up extra trump and discarding your weakest card. On the minus side, our indecisive and often cautious group often stuck the dealer, which meant that the dealer had to make a decision because none of the rest of us wanted to. We euchred each other all the time, so the opposite team often won when we stuck the dealer. Only those of us from the Midwest played euchre, but we had taught it to everyone in the program on the first overnight trip we'd had. It felt like a long time ago, but it had really only been a matter of months since we met.

There was something about having a very limited friend group that you saw all day every day that pulled you together. Familiarity breeds contempt, but not when you're only going to have a handful of months together.

All of us had naturally split into groups. There was a group of girls all from New England who went to prestigious colleges, and they kept to themselves. There was another group of blondes that went to a local bar every day after school. My group was made up of the people who didn't want to die of cirrhosis, and all of us were friendly. Lauren drank like a fish, and it would have been more natural for Fitz to fall into the bar fly group. However, Fitz had ended up with us. She had a distaste for alcohol and drank it sparingly a handful of times a year. Even though my group went out, it had never been a problem for her. Fitz stuck to virgin Cuba Libres (also known as plain Coke), and she had fun dancing with the rest of us. Her flame-red hair made her stick out in the sea of dark-haired Ecuadorians, and she got almost as much attention as the blondes, who came out with us sometimes. Her green-blue eyes didn't hurt. They were called ojos claros here, and sometimes they were called ojos sajones. Only the Germans had them, and they were lost in the first generation of mestizo. As such, they were highly prized and considered overwhelmingly attractive.

Fitz didn't look like a prize right now, though. She was swigging Coke from the bottle like her life depended on it. It had been a long day, and it seemed that you didn't need to have alcohol to need a drink after a long day. Catie dealt all of us in, I set up the score cards for the two teams, and we got down to it.

Catie was easy to read, and so was Fitz. Alice was the hardest person to play with, because she had a beautiful poker face. She could have a loner, and you'd never tell. Fitz was not like that at all. You could see her get visibly excited the instant that she looked at her hand. She was my weathercock for how good the other team's hands were. Whenever she got a loner, she bounced up and down. I always knew that I needed to call trump before the call went to her.

Catie and I worked together wonderfully. She was all on the surface. None of us allowed table talk, so Catie and I had worked out a system of physical actions to say what we had. We'd brush invisible dirt off of our shoulders when we had spades. We twirled our hair when we had diamonds. We stretched out our fingers when we had hearts. Clubs was indicated by tucking hair behind our ears.

It was almost like kemps, if any other euchre partners had worked out a system like that. None of them were as clever as us, though, so Catie and I took names and kicked ass every time that we played together. In real life, Catie and I wouldn't be as close. In this strange pseudo-reality, which was both real and unreal, Catie and I were as close as two people could be basically right after meeting. Catie was easy for me to be with.

We went through the rounds of euchre very quickly. Our group simply cleared the board as soon as we knew how many points we were getting. As soon as someone had three tricks and someone else had a stopper, we just chalked up a point on our scorecards and shuffled for the next round. Catie and I won the first round of euchre, of course. The cards were against the second round, though, and we lost 8-10 to Alice and Fitz. Fitz was hyped up on sugar and caffeine. Alice had solid game on.

With all that though, Catie and I won the last round of euchre. I held my cards when Catie held her hand out for them, so that she could shuffle again.

"I think that's enough for tonight. We have to be at the tour office early tomorrow."

Catie sighed. "I guess. Here, let me put it away, then." She collected all the cards in the deck, and she put them into her case. "I call the bathroom." She got her bag of toiletries, and she walked into our tiny shared bathroom. You had to walk all the way inside before you closed the door, because otherwise you'd find yourself standing on the wrong side of the door, back in the shared bedroom.

Alice went over to her bed and flopped down. "Oh, God. Do we have to wake up early tomorrow?"

"Yes, we do. But it's ok. I mean, you can sleep on the car ride out. It's not going to be a big deal."

"Ugh! I hate waking up so *early*."

"I wake up at 5 AM every morning to go running with Lauren," Fitz said.

Alice opened one eye. "That's because you're a maniac. No offense."

"None taken. It just takes more discipline." She started stripping. Americans were far more prudish in America. After we'd stripped down in front of each other in the Galapagos, we got much more comfortable changing in front of each other. Fitz was also much less concerned about her body than the rest of us. She had a runner's physique, the heavy leg muscles and the bony ribcage sticking out. She ate a lot, not as much as Lauren of course, but she looked like she existed on a diet of carrot sticks alone.

I turned my back to her, and I put on my running shorts and the old Mathletes shirt that I used as sleepwear. "I'll set my alarm so that we have plenty of time to go to the office right as it opens."

Alice sighed. "Ok."

Catie left the bathroom, and Fitz went to brush her teeth and remove her minimal makeup. I tapped Alice's shoulder. "I think that you'll be more comfortable under the sheets."

Without opening her eyes, she said, "That would require moving."

"Well, yes."

"I don't think that I have the energy for that right now."

"Hey, it was your great idea to go walking around town with just Fitz," I teased.

"I know." She blew out a breath. "It seemed like a good idea at the time, but we got up early today, and we've done so much."

I nodded. "We have." I went to my bed and laid down. "We only have so much time in Ecuador, though. We might as well run around the Amazon while we're here, you know?"

Alice yawned and stretched. "Yeah. Well, whatever. Wake me up tomorrow morning when I have to get up." She began breathing deeply, in a slow rhythm that told me she was basically sleep.

When Fitz got out of the bathroom, I went in to quickly use some cleanser and brush my teeth. I had bought travel covers for my toothbrush at Walmart before I left the United States. It turned out to be a good investment; because we traveled so much, we basically always needed a spare toothbrush. I kept one in the duffel bag that I took on our weekend trips, and I kept the one that I used during the week at home. Doubtless my host mom would be horrified by my lack of hygiene if she ever noticed, but I had an ensuite bathroom to myself. Probably the only person who would have noticed was the maid, and she had the weekends off.

When I came out, Fitz was under the covers. She had somehow maneuvered Alice under the covers, probably by use of brute force. Catie was in our bed, reading Pedro Paramo.

I slid under the covers. "Is it any good?" I yawned.

"It's ok. It seems like they are in hell. I don't know. They talk about the heat constantly."

"Fascinating," I said drily. "Could you turn off the light when you're done?"

Ever considerate, she turned it off entirely. I knew that she would have problems falling asleep tonight after the shock of today, but I just couldn't keep my eyes open anymore. Fitz was snoring, and Alice's deep breaths were the white noise soundtrack I needed to fall asleep.

OCELOTS AND GUINEA PIGS

The next morning, we headed to the office as it opened. A battered van with faded paint took us to the Puyo rescue center. Amazonian animals were often captured and used as pets. However, wild Amazonian animals did not make that great of pets. They weren't domesticated like cats and dogs. When people found out about exotic animals living in the urban areas, the animals were confiscated and taken to the rescue center.

There were a ton of animals, some of which I had never seen before. I had seen alligators from a distance in the Everglades in Florida, but I got to see caimans up close. They were smaller cousins, and they were faster, too. I was pretty sure I could fight one, though, if it came down to it.

The Amazon held a large variety of monkeys. You couldn't see them that often in the wild, because most of them knew better than to stick around humans. The best way to see them was in zoos or rescue centers. They were tiny things, and their shrieks were painful to hear.

My favorites were the ocelots, which were very small big cats or very large house cats. The pattern of their pelts helped them fade into the shadows.

The guide shook his finger at them. "These two, they are troublemakers."

"Troublemakers how?" I asked. They just looked like two content kitties to me. They were licking themselves and sitting in the sun. A half-eaten rodent was in their cage.

"They escape all the time." The guide shook his head. "They have no need for food, but they go hunting anyway."

"What is there to hunt? And isn't that more trouble than cats normally go through? I thought that the cat was the only animal who behaved perfectly rationally?"

"Not ocelots. I think they enjoy stirring the pot. They are great climbers, and they climb the trees and leap outside of the enclosure. They go to the chicken coops of the local families, and they eat their chicks." He sighed. "We feed them more food than they need, and instead of getting fat and happy, they run off."

"It's part of ocelot nature to hunt and chase, though," I pointed out reasonably. "Do you ever let them hunt?"

"I don't run the rescue center, but that's a good point. I will talk to my friend Eduardo when I see him next." He cleared his throat. "The ocelots are the last thing that we'll see here. We will go to the cabins, freshen up, and have lunch now. Follow me, please."

He lead the way back to the van, and all of us went back inside of it. Alice dozed off immediately. You'd think that she hadn't had eight hours of sleep, even though she'd had more than that. Catie stared out the window, and Fitz took out her crochet hook and made a hat. You wouldn't peg Fitz as an arts and crafts kind of girl, but she was constantly in motion. If she didn't have something occupying her hands, she fidgeted a lot. She had to stay in motion or drive the rest of us insane.

When we arrived at the camp, all four of us took our things to the cabin. We were sharing one, and it had two single beds and one double.

"Catie and I will take the double. You guys can have the single."

Alice nodded, and she went to the bathroom to splash water on her face.

"I'm hungry," Fitz said. "I'm going to figure out where lunch is."

"Right behind you," Catie said.

"I'm waiting for Alice. I'll catch up with you guys later." Catie and Fitz left.

Alice got out of the bathroom. "Do you have any pads?"

"I have Always. Does that work?"

"Yeah, that's fine. I think I might be starting my period right now."

"Ugh, that's always a pain. I guess you should go swimming in the river, just in case the piranhas get you."

She rolled her eyes. "Yeah, I'll definitely watch out for the fish that can strip a man to the bone in seconds. Piranhas get a bad rap."

"I know. Let's go eat lunch, ok?" She grabbed her camera, sprayed bug spray on every inch of herself, and headed out of our cabin.

The smell of frying fish lead us to another cabin. It was more like a lodge, and it was much bigger than the cabin we were in. Fitz and Catie were already sitting down.

"Mm, that smells good."

Catie made a face. "It's always fish."

"Sweetie, they eat locally sourced food. In the Amazon, and in fact in most places that can't afford beef and other meat, fish is the primary source of protein. You know this. You understand basic anthropology. Fish have been a major source of protein for a very long time now."

"I wish I could eat a huge steak."

"We'll go out for steak when we go back to Quito, I promise." I winked at her. "But for now, let's just focus on putting something in our stomachs before we run around this afternoon, ok?"

Catie sat back. "Ok."

Fitz was eating a banana. "I'm starving." She took a huge bite.

"How did you even get that banana? Isn't it all bruised?"

She swallowed. "I didn't bring it. They gave it to me when they saw my face. That was a smart move. I probably look like I'm about to eat someone."

"Not after eating the banana," I said.

Alice yawned. "I can't believe it's only lunchtime. Seriously, we need to get more sleep at night if we're going to travel this much around Ecuador."

"Noted." Right then, a short, dark-skinned lady came out with a pitcher of white guanabana smoothies. She poured a little into each of our cups, nodded, and left the pitcher.

I drained my cup, and I immediately poured another. Fitz drained hers, and I passed her the pitcher so that she could drink some more.

"I think the smoothies are going to be the most I eat today," Catie said. "Could you pass it, please, Fitz?"

"Ya," Fitz said. She turned the pitcher around so that the handle faced Catie, and she pushed it across. "Here you go."

"You're going to have to get used to eating fish," I told Catie. "Seriously, it's like every meal here. Most people can't afford livestock."

"Easy for you to say," Catie snorted. "You've eaten all kinds of fish. My family eats chicken and stuff for dinner, not fish. We are not cool cats like you."

Fitz sighed. "I can't believe I'm saying this, but Catie, you need to play nice." Catie frowned, and she crossed her arms. I couldn't believe it, but she was sulking like a toddler.

The food came out, carried by the same cocinera who had come out before with the guanabana smoothies. She served each of us a fish filet. She went back into the kitchen to take out a big pot of rice. She gave each of us a spoonful, and she left the container on the table with us.

Fitz dug in. With a full mouth, she said, "Where's our guide?"

"I guess he's not joining us for lunch." I shrugged. "Whatever, we have to spend the next two days with him. I'm sure we'll see him a lot. Do you guys remember what comes after lunch?"

"We're swimming in a waterfall," Catie chimed in. "I hope it's not cold like that time we went rappelling down a waterfall in Mindo the first time we went there."

"We were in the mountains, then, Catie," Alice snapped. "This time, the water's not ice melt."

"No need to get snippy," Fitz cut in. "I was worried about the same thing. I guess the water is warmer in the Amazon."

We ate our fish and rice in silence. Right as we finished, our guide showed up. "Ah, excellent. All of you are done. If you could change into your bathing suits, we can head to the waterfall. It is a two-hour boat ride."

Catie choked. "Excuse me? Did you say two hours?"

The tour guide nodded. "Yes. It's two hours. Is that a problem?"

"No problem," I cut in quickly. "Our boat rides between the islands in the Galapagos took more than that."

"But we were in an archipelago!" Catie whined. "We're on the mainland now."

The guide shrugged. "You can only navigate inside of the Amazon by boat. There are no roads here. Even if we built them, they'd only wash out quickly. The petroleros have to repave the roads that they have to the oil wells every month, if not sooner. The equipment they move is expensive, and it can get damaged by a bumpy road. This is the Amazon."

Catie looked even unhappier. "Fine. I just hope I don't get boat sick."

The tour guide started the motor. All of us put on orange life jackets, and we stepped into the little boat. When I looked behind us, I could see oil spewing into the river, polluting it. It was disgusting and terrible, but boats were truly the only way to navigate a literal jungle.

I couldn't believe it, but Alice fell asleep again. I was a little worried that she had narcolepsy. Catie was humming to herself quietly, and Fitz was watching the greenery zoom by us while tapping her fingers on her thigh. We couldn't talk over the noise of the boat, and so I just let my mind wander as I looked around.

In our anthropology class, we had talked about the potential for income that biomedicine presented. Lipitor was found in the Amazon, based on ancient remedies. There was more than one pharmaceutical company that was looking for a similar plant, something that the indigenous people knew about and the Western world didn't. The three of us who were in a biomedicine class at PUCE-Quito said that there were three representatives from Pfizer who were learning from their professor, an Amazonian shaman's daughter. Shamen were known are yachajs here, translated as wise ones. The j made a k sound. It didn't make sense to me, but a lot of pronunciation in kichwa did not make a ton of sense to me. Native kichwa speakers used a weird sound whenever there was a double l in a Spanish word. There were a limited amount of words in English that had the same sound; million was one. For example, a botella had the weird sound; it was said bo-tel-ya by kichwa speakers instead of bo-te-ya by a normal Quiteño.

The three girls in the biomedicine class had been able to witness something that our anthropology professor -- one of them, anyway -- had given us a paper on. In Ecuador, guinea pigs were native. They were rodents, yeah, but they were gigantic. People ate them, just like rabbits. In a world where domesticated meat was too expensive for normal people to eat, guinea pigs, called cuy and pronounced kwee, were a major source of food in the Andes and basically anywhere someone could catch a guinea pig for along enough to kill it and eat it.

In indigenous medicine, they were used just as an X-ray machine would be used in a normal hospital. They took a poor guinea pig the opposite gender of the patient, and they shook the tiny little thing all over the body of the invalid. Then, they'd cut up the guinea pig to find out what was wrong inside of the patient. Its stomach had been malformed, and the shaman's daughter had treated the patient with a stomach-centered cure. One of the three girls had cried, and after that none of them could even see roasted guinea pig without looking a little green. Roasted guinea pig was every-where, especially in restaurants that carried normal Ecuadorian food.

While guinea pig X-rays were not going to make their way to the United States anytime soon, the potential of biomedicine was going to shake up the pharmaceutical industry. The entire jungle was full of plants that weren't categorized. They estimated that there were millions of different species of plants and animals that had never been encountered before by mankind. I was seeing them zoom by as I sat in this Amazon-polluting boat with our tour guide.

SACRED CAVES

When we finally got to the waterfall, Alice woke up. "What time is it?" she asked softly.

"It's time to go swimming!" the tour guide told us cheerfully. Alice grimaced as if she had a stomachache. We got out of the boat, and we could see the towering waterfall next to us.

"Take off your shoes, but be careful on the rocks," the tour guide cautioned us. "They are slippery when they are wet."

"This is a waterfall," I said. "They are always wet."

"Precisely," he said.

All of us took off our shoes. Catie led the way into the water. "It's warm!" she exclaimed.

The water was brown; it wasn't like walking into a swimming pool or the ocean. The Amazon has sedimentary rivers, and we were basically swimming around in diluted mud. However, it was still pretty cool, because we were swimming in the Amazon, the source of exotic documentaries back home. There were fish that we couldn't see swimming around us, and the waterfall was as gorgeous as the one in Peguche, which was sacred to the Andean indigenous people. We went in one by one.

"Do you want to go into a sacred cave?" the tour guide asked once all of us were in the water.

The four of us looked at each other. "Yeah."

"Go under the waterfall. Quickly, now." He passed through it first. I felt like we were going through a magic door into another world. I went in right after him, and the other girls followed me through. Behind the waterfall, there was a cave that stretched into the emptiness. It was dark, although a little bit of sunlight made it through the waterfall. The tour guide had a waterproof flashlight.

"Be careful. The rocks --"

"Are wet. Got it." Fitz sped up and got to the front. "What makes it sacred?"

"What makes anything sacred?" the tour guide asked us. "Human belief, that's all. There's a legend that there are dragons who live in this cave."

"Dragons?" Catie piped up. "Why would there be dragons in the Amazon?"

"I don't know," the tour guide said, "but there are tales of giant dragons here. They are supposed to be purple. They are only seen at night."

"So we're safe, then?" Fitz joked. She didn't hold with scaredy-cat nonsense. Catie got closer to me, and I tucked my arm in hers. No dragons were going to get her while I was there, even if they were local folklore based on dinosaur fossils. The purple part was weird, though. Maybe it was part of drinking ayahuasca.

"It's ok, Catie. I got you."

"I'm fine." There was a small echo in the cave. Her hand on my arm tightened, though, and I knew that she was scared to be in the dark. She always kept hostel doors open a crack. She was a little old to be afraid of monsters, but there was always a scared child inside of all of us.

"What is there to do inside of the cave?" I asked our tour guide.

"Not much. There are bugs." He shined his light around us. We could see Gollum-covered insects.

"Oh my gosh," Fitz said. "These are disgusting." She crouched down to take a closer look in the beam from the flashlight. "They're so big!"

Catie's hand was now cutting off my circulation. I hadn't had someone hold my hand this tight since that time when I took my cousin on a roller coaster ride. She's 3 times as acrophobic as I am. "Can we go back?" I heard the tremor in her voice that signaled danger.

"Yeah, of course." I patted her arm. "Let's go back through the waterfall where there's sunlight."

"Ok, we'll see you guys out there," Alice said as we walked towards the dim light at the entrance. She crouched next to Fitz. I had no idea that they were into entomology, but they seemed as fascinated by the variety of gross bugs as the pretty hummingbirds we saw in Mindo before Gabriella died.

Catie was slowing down, and she was breathing funny. "Chill, honey," I told her. "We're almost there." I pulled her through the waterfall, and she sputtered as we got through the other side.

"Are you ok?"

She was choking. She breathed hard to catch her breath, and she braced her hands on her thighs as she bent over. "Fine." She spat out some water. "It's fine. I'm fine."

"That was creepy, eh?" I asked her.

"Creepy is an understatement. Why would a sacred cave be covered with giant, pale bugs? Couldn't they find something better to worship?"

"Honey, it's the Amazon. It's not like they're going to drive 10 minutes to go to Mass every day. You should respect the indigenous culture; it's definitely valuable to learn about different faith systems."

"Worshipping the Pachamama, the Earth, in a cave full of disgusting bugs and god knows what else is not my idea of religious ceremonies." Catie was splashing herself with water now, and she was scrubbing the mud off of her feet. It was a futile task, since the entire river was diluted mud. It would make her feel better, though, to tell herself that she was clean, so I didn't say anything. People have an endless ability to delude themselves. Frankly there wasn't much that I could give to Catie in the middle of the Amazon that would make her feel clean and safe.

I could see Fitz coming out from under the waterfall, bursting through like it was nothing. Alice was right behind her, the Eurydice to Fitz's Orpheus. The guide brought up the rear. He turned off his flashlight when he was through.

"We will leave soon," he told us. "We're expected in a kichwa community. They will paint your faces with achiote, red paint, and they will show you how they make clay pots from river clay. They will also show you how to use blow darts."

"Will there be curare?" Fitz asked. I could tell from the gleam in her eyes and the tone of her voice that she looked forward to tangling with the deadly poison.

"No. It is getting harder and harder to find the vine to make curare, and we buy whatever meat we eat. Well, they do."

"You weren't born in the Amazon, were you?"

The tour guide laughed. "No, I wasn't. I was born in Puyo, but I've been here my entire life. I might as well belong to the rain forest."

KICHWA COMMUNITY

*C*atie was eager to get away from the terrifying dragon cave, and she was the first one in the boat. It swayed as she stepped in, and the horrible smell of the motor wafted out when the tour guide started it. It only took us a half hour to get to the kichwa community. I was sure that it would be longer without a motor and only a paddle, but the nice thing about the Amazon was that everything was alongside the river system.

When we got out, we saw all of the houses that were on stilts. No houses were built on the ground. There were solar panels all around us.

"There's a government program to provide solar panels to Amazon residents," the tour guide said. "It is impossible to having a traditional electrical grid in the Amazon, so every homestead here is self-sufficient. There's certainly enough sunlight to provide for each family."

"That's good." I walked around and looked at the solar panels on top of the shed. They were hooked up to a battery that was on a small, battered wood table. I could smell smoke. "What's burning?"

"It's the fire."

I felt my eyebrows scrunch over my nose. "A fire? Isn't it warm enough here? It's the Amazon."

"There's more than one reason to have a fire. It's a cooking fire, and it also serves to keep the mosquitos away."

"Isn't that what bug spray's for?" Catie interjected. I knew that as soon as we got back to the cabins, she would be slathering herself in it. This trip had a little too much nature in it for a girl raised in the United States.

"Bug spray." The tour guide snorted. "There's something much better that is all natural." He led us further into the homestead. "Do you see the large gray clump in the fire?"

"Yeah," all of us chorused.

"It's a termite hive."

"Ew!" Catie said. She looked like she was going to hurl. "That's disgusting."

"The termite hive is the reason that you're not being eaten alive by mosquitos right now, so have some respected," the tour guide chided. "It's natural mosquito repellant, and it doesn't poison the ecosystem like DDT."

"Why is it in the fire?" Fitz asked.

"Something about the smoke keeps the mosquitos away," the tour guide replied. "Anyway, sit down so that the lady can show you how to make clay pots.

All four of us sat down on a log around the fire, and the tour guide crouched next to us. An indigenous women with gray hair and wrinkles was sitting next to a wooden board with fat rolls of clay on it, like little snakes. She took each one of them and rolled them out to be thinner and longer. She stacked each piece on top of the other to form a bowl. Instead of the smoothly curved bowl that could get lopsided when you threw it on a pottery wheel, she just had stacks upon stacks. It looked like a children's game, but she was much more precise about it. She slowly built her bowl from the little snakes, and it looked like something you could eat out of. Watching her build the clay pot deliberately was interesting, but it couldn't capture Fitz's attention for long. I saw her look at a tiny little girl who was hiding behind the stilts of her house. She had huge eyes, and she was such a cute little girl. I didn't want to scare her away, but Fitz had no problems walking over to the house and saying, "Hello."

The little girl laughed and then ran away to the solar shed. She'd probably never seen anyone with hair the color of fire before.

"What's her name?" Fitz asked the guide.

"Ninasisa," he replied. "She's 3."

"She looks younger. She's cute."

"She is." The lady had finished making her bowl, and she was setting it on the wood plank that used to hold the fat clay snakes. "What happens now?" In the United States, in the midst of Western civilization, she would fire the bowl in a kiln. In the middle of the Amazonian rain forest, where there was no electrical grid and limited electricity, I had no idea if her homestead could even support a kiln, let alone afford one.

"I'll ask." The tour guide spoke in kichwa to the lady. The lady replied.

"She says that you leave the bowl in the sun for three days. Then, it is ready."

That was interesting. It was fascinating to me that people stilled lived the simplest kind of life. "Tell her thank you, please."

The guide said something to her. She smiled and looked at me. She nodded and smiled shyly. I smiled back. There were some things that could convey meaning without any shared language, and a smile was one of them.

BLOW

"**W**ell, now that we are done with the bowl part, would you like to paint your face with achiote and use a blowpipe?"

Fitz stood up. "*Yes!* I want to go first." The guide got a huge blowpipe out of the house, and he gave it to Fitz. It was more than a meter long, and it was black.

"Come here." The guide gestured towards the back of the homestead. There was a fake bird sitting there. "Use this for target practice."

Fitz filled up her lungs -- runner's lungs -- and she blew as hard as she could. The blowdart fell into the ground, many feet away from the fake bird. Fitz frowned. She was the most athletic one of all of us. "Let me try again."

She picked up another tiny blow dart, but it in, and blew hard. This one almost hit the fake bird, but this wasn't horseshoes. Close didn't count.

"Let me try, Fitz." Alice tugged gently on the blowpipe. It was a good thing that we had gotten comfortable with each other; we were each going to put our mouth on a blow pipe that had been used by countless people. It was hardly the golden standard of hygiene, but then again, there was not much that you could expect in the depths of the Amazon, far away from where civilization could easily reach. Alice's attempt was a lot like Fitz's second attempt. It got close to the bird, but she didn't pierce it.

"Let me try." Alice handed the blowpipe over to Catie. Catie blew it with enthusiasm but no aim. The blowdart shot out of the pipe and dug itself into the ground. I didn't think that anyone would be able to pull it out.

Catie put the pipe down. "Your turn, Jade. Let's see how good you are at using a blowpipe.

I picked it up. It was heavier than it looked. It was almost solid wood, except for the very center where the dart went. I took in a deep breath, the kind that yoga teachers tell you to take, aimed at the fake bird, and slammed out my air.

The dart hit the little fake bird square in the middle. The other three girls burst into applause.

"Way to go, Jade!" Catie took the blowpipe back. "I want to try again." This time, she got as close as Alice had gotten. Using a blowpipe was much harder than it looked, because you had to balance the blowpipe while you aimed it and blew.

"How come it was so easy for you?" Fitz asked. "None of the rest of us could do it."

"I do yoga." I shrugged. "I also used to balloon. Without a pump, you have to use your own breath."

"Balloon...as in balloon animals?"

"Yeah. I thought that it would be a fun thing to learn how to do when I was younger, and so I was in an after-school program that taught me how to create fun balloon shapes. I think that my mom was grateful when I stopped. She never got over jumping anytime that a balloon popped. I still have my old balloons and my pump though. They're somewhere in my bedroom back home."

"Wow," Fitz said. "I used to play flute, and I thought that I had really good breath control. Yours is really good though."

"Whatever. It's a combination of breath control and the ability to aim a huge piece of wood."

"That's what she said." All of us laughed.

The guide let us sit there for a half minute, but kichwa time was over. "We need to go back to the boat. We should make it back to the cabins before dark. We can go on a nature hike after dark, but it's hard to navigate a boat when the sun is down."

"Ok." Catie hightailed it back to the boat. The rest of us carefully got in, and the guide started up the smelly motor to take us back to the cabins.

The boat ride out to the waterfall had taken two hours, but the homestead must have been on the way back. It didn't take 2 hours to get to the cabins. The sun was beginning to slip down by the time that we got to the cabins.

SHOWERS

"*D*inner is in an hour. If you want to take a shower, I suggest doing it now. All of the water heaters are solar powered, so if you want to bathe at night, it will be very cold."

"Dibs!" Alice said.

"Second," Catie called.

Fitz and I looked at each other and shrugged. I didn't mind being a little bit grubby; it wasn't like there were any cute guys in the middle of nowhere in the Amazon rain forest. Fitz was pretty enough, but she wasn't self-conscious about her looks. She preferred to earn her keep by achieving things. One day, I was sure, she'd be the CEO of a company of badasses. She was the one out of all of us who was going to do just fine roughing it. She didn't need a shower or running water at all.

"I'll go third, but don't rush, Alice and Catie." I crossed my arms. "I can just be disgusting and gross."

"Good," Alice said.

"I'll hurry," Catie promised. "I think proper hygiene is important."

Alice went into the cabin, got a spare set of clothes, and hopped into the bathroom. Catie got all of her shower stuff ready, so that she could be in and out as fast as humanly possible. Catie and I always shared shampoo and toothpaste on trips; it cut down on us having to remember it. She always carried it, though I was the one who had paid for it. It worked out for us. Catie came off as a ditz, but she was a good planner. Now that Gabriella was gone, she was the next best thing that we had.

Alice was out in record time, despite what she had said. Catie practically ran into the shower, and I could imagine her rigorously bathing herself so that I could get in. It really wasn't a big deal to me; skipping a day of showering was not going to kill me.

"Are you sure you don't care, Fitz? I could go last if you wanted."

"I've showered in colder water than you'd ever find in the Amazon. If you think this is bad, you haven't seen anything. I'll either go without or deal with it. It's really not a big deal," Fitz assured me.

"Ok, then." Catie walked out of the bathroom, and I went in. There was our two-in-one shampoo on the shower floor. I lathered it and used it as body wash. It wasn't ideal, but it was the best that I was going to be able to do right then. I wasn't too sticky from running around in that muddy waterfall, and so it didn't take too much time to get clean. I felt a lot better when I was putting on my fresh clothes. Maybe it was a female thing, but there was something fundamentally satisfying about putting on a clean set of clothing. I walked out.

"Fitz, I am sure that you have time to shower before dinner."

Fitz went in, and I heard the shower go. "Do you guys want to go on the nature hike?"

Alice yawned. "Nah. We've been on the go a lot, and we've seen a ton of stuff today. I'm good with what I've got."

"Me, too." Catie was laying on a bed with her feet dangling off. "I just want to go to sleep after dinner. Travel is exhausting, and we've been in boats so much in Ecuador."

"True. I want to go on the hike, though."

"See if Fitz will go with you."

"I feel like it's the kind of thing that she'd be up for. We'll see." I dug around in my backpack and put my camera in my pocket.

Fitz came out of the bathroom. "What? I thought I heard my name."

"You did. Do you want to go on the after dark nature hike that he offered us?"

"Nah," Fitz said. "I'd rather look at it in books. It seems really cool to walk around the Amazon and see all the things that you've only read about, but then when you see it in person it's just a bunch of leaves."

Catie laughed. "That's true."

"I might be going on my own, then." I didn't mind.

"Are you sure?" Catie asked. "I can go if you want me to."

"No," I reassured her. "I am a big girl. I can wander around the rain forest behind a guy with a machete. Between the two of us, I'm pretty sure we could outsmart an ocelot or whatever."

"Ocelots can't eat humans," Fitz corrected. "I'm pretty sure that chickens are about their maximum when it comes to killing things."

"Maybe. But you can never be too careful. Promise me that you'll be careful in the dark."

"I'll be careful." I laughed. "What's the worst that could happen? I'll watch out for big purple dragons."

All of us laughed.

DINNER AND DESSERT

*D*inner was baked fish wrapped up in a big leaf. This was actually common in Vietnam, so I couldn't be happier. As soon as I finished up my fish, Catie swapped her plate with mine.

I protested. "I can't eat two whole fish. Alice, do you want to go halfsies with me?" Most of her plate was clean.

"I can eat two whole fish. Give me some, please." Fitz pushed her completely clean plate towards me. I split Catie's fish into three parts and shared it equally between the three of us.

"Catie, take some of my rice, please. I know that you don't like fish, but you have to eat something." I took some of the rice and put it on her plate.

Catie smiled. "Yes, Mama," Catie snarked. She was used to my protective instincts, though.

"None of your sass, now." I winked. I wasn't even Southern, but I could do a Southern mother impression like none other.

"I hope they have dessert." Fitz belched. "Scuse me."

"Gross, Fitz." Alice finished up the last of Catie's fish. "I could do with some dessert, too, though."

Fitz went to the kitchen to look for more food. She came back with a basket of fresh fruit. "Here, guys."

"Oh my god, you are wonderful. Did she speak Spanish after all?"

"No. I used pantomime to convey my meaning. I think that I do a good impression of a starving man."

Catie, Alice, and I laughed. Fitz was a huge ham, and she was subtly one of the funniest people in our group. "What do we have?"

"Bananas, because it's Ecuador. I also have a papaya. Do any of you know how to cute a papaya?"

"First of all, do you have a knife?"

"Yeah, she put one into the basket. I think that she likes me."

"Whatever. I can try to cut the papaya if you give it to me." I took the knife, and I cut the papaya in half like I'd seen my parents do whenever we had papaya at home. I cut out the seedy center, and I cut the rest of the papaya in big chunks. All of us reused our dinner forks to eat fruit. I think that we wouldn't normally be too fancy to use our hands, but fruit was pretty sticky with juice. It was not a good idea to get too grubby in the Amazon, because if you weren't careful, you would end up with sticky fingers for a while. It wasn't like it was advisable to suck on your fingers to clean them here. We finished all of the bananas and the papaya.

"I'm full," Catie announced. "I'm going back to the cabin and passing out."

"Right behind you," Alice and Fitz chorused.

"I'm going to find the guide. I want to see what I can see."

"Good luck! Do you have your camera?"

I patted my pocket. "Right here."

"Good. Take pictures so that the rest of us can live vicariously through you."

"Aye, aye, captain."

CHICHA AND NATURE HIKE

I walked around the little set of cabins. In a tiny room in the lodge, I found the guide drinking chicha with the cocinera. He stopped drinking, and he wiped his mouth. "Ah, you are done with dinner?"

"Yes. I'd like to go on that nature hike, if you are still up for that."

"Yes, of course. It's part of your tour package. Where are the other girls? We should get going as soon as possible so that we can see as much as we can before we need to head back."

"They aren't coming. It's just the two of us."

"And my machete. I'll get my flashlight, and I'll meet you in front of the lodge in 5 minutes, un ratito, ok?"

"Ok."

I went to go sit down at the doorstep of the lodge. He didn't take long to get ready. He came out. "Ready, ya?"

"Ya." It was a really weird mix of German influence and possibly kichwa influence that everyone said ya instead of yes or sí.

"Let's go." He had a huge flashlight, much bigger than the one that he had brought to go to the cave. I guessed it wasn't waterproof enough to take on that adventure. It cast an enormous ray of light. It was going to scare away all of the wildlife, but that's why we were calling it a nature hike. Nature was going to be light on actual fauna and heavy on the flora, because it couldn't run away from humans. He took his machete in one hand and used the flashlight in the other. "Do you see the frogs?"

We were barely out of the encampment. I think I would notice if I was surrounded by frogs.

"No."

"Look harder."

I looked harder. Right at the edges of where the light from the flashlight fell, I could see little glitters. There were tiny eyes on the plants. When I tried to get closer, the little glints moved. And then I realized that the frogs were all camouflaged to fit in perfectly in the rain forest.

"Pretty, no?"

"Yeah, the frogs are really pretty."

"Here's the secret: the prettier the frogs are, the more poisonous they are."

"What?"

"Yeah, every major predator in the Amazon knows that a brightly colored frog means that you steer away. They will kill you."

"Those tiny things? I mean, those frogs are the size of my hand. My thumb. It's like not there's much to them."

"It take a drop of poison to kill a man. But keep going, I can show you more plants." He hiccuped.

"Are you drunk?"

"Drunk? What is drunk? Have I had chicha? Yes." He hacked at a nearby vine outside of the path with his machete. "There is no drunk in the Amazon rain forest. But hey, if you want to take this nature walk by yourself, I'll go home. There's nothing out here but mud and plants."

"I mean, you just pointed out all the frogs."

He snorted. "The frogs. There always frogs. This is the Amazon." He burped. "All the tourists love the frogs, and I always ruin their dreams of owning one by telling them how dangerous pretty frogs are. Pretty frogs are like pretty girls. Good to look at, but not good to touch."

Ok, he'd obviously had quite a lot to drink with the cocinera. "Can we go back now?"

"Sure, sure, whatever you want, Chinita. We'll go back." He turned around, and we headed back the way that we came, a trail marked by vines that he'd hacked through with his machete. All of a sudden, he stopped.

"Oh, look, there is one of your precious little frogs right there, Chinita. Do you want to hold it?"

"No," I said sharply. "They are poisonous. I just want to go back to camp."

"Oh, it's such a little thing," he mocked. "Surely it can't hurt a full-sized human?" He picked it up, and he brandished it at me. "Scared, Chinita?"

"Put it down."

"No. It moves me." He kissed its back. The frog did not like being squeezed and shaken. It was clearly struggling to get out of the guide's hand.

"I don't feel so good." The guide's machete, fell out of his hand. The flashlight rolled away and get into a puddle. "I think you need to get help." He staggered forward, and I watched helplessly as he fall on top of his machete, which pierced him completely through. I didn't know how it had enough force to push through him; it must have been purely his body weight and the angle.

"Oh, my god!" I went to get the flashlight, but I pushed it further into the puddle. I wasn't as bad as Alice when it came to directions, but I was in the middle of the rain forest with my guide dead at my feet, no machete, no flashlight. Suddenly, I was quite a lot more afraid of the fauna than I had been before.

Right behind my shoulder, there was a voice. "Hello."

HELLO

I jumped a foot.

"What the hell?"

"Are you lost?"

I was pretty sure that the answer was self-evident. "I'm pretty sure I am." I was in the middle of the effing Amazon, alone except for this weird creeper. My alarm bells would be ringing a lot harder in Quito, but there were a lot more sketchy people in the cities than there were out in the boonies. Something about being isolated from other people made humans more cooperative. "Who are you?"

"I'll help you find shelter for tonight. Well, we will, with some conditions."

"Who is we?"

"My brother and I."

"What are your conditions?"

"Stay the night with us." I felt his breath on my neck, and I shivered involuntarily.

"Buddy, I'd rather get eaten by a fictitious purple dragon than go anywhere with you and your brother. Thanks, but no thanks. I'll take my chances with the poison frogs."

"Are you sure? There are many things that can see you at night. A purple dragon might be the nicest of them."

I felt a lot like Snow White in the woods after the Huntsman spared her life and told her to run. I felt like every tree held a hungry jaguar just waiting to pounce. I was soft, easy meat. I didn't have a weapon, and I wasn't going to take the machete out of my guide's dead body.

I could choose to stay in the middle of the Amazon and hope that someone from the camp found me -- unlikely -- or I could go with this guy now and exchange a night for the rest of my life.

"How far away is your shelter?"

"Not very."

"I can't see very well," I warned. "And I have no idea where we are going."

"That's not a problem. Hook your hand in my belt, and I'll lead you on a safe path." He took my hand, kissed it, and put it on his belt. His courtly manners were incongruous with the way that we met, but it made me think that he wasn't a total barbarian. I held on tightly as he began to move with tons of confidence through the underbrush. Even the guide had needed a machete to get through the tangle of vines. This guy didn't duck or need a machete; it seemed like he knew exactly how to move through the jungle. I was perfectly safe right behind him, stepping quickly and careful in the muddy Amazon.

After 5 minutes, he said, "In here." He ducked, and I ducked, too. I couldn't even really see, but I could sense his motion. I could feel the floor change. It was a bunch of wet rock.

"Is this a hidden river?"

"Yeah, the Amazon is riddled with hidden rivers. There's so much water. Be careful. The rock --"

"Is wet. Ok. Do you have a flashlight or something?"

"No, I don't have a flashlight. Just keep your hand on my belt."

He picked up speed, and I had to try hard to keep up with him on the slippery rock. "You're very slow." He wasn't winded at all, and I was panting.

"Way to add insult to injury, buddy. I'm slow, ok?"

"You don't have to be." He picked me up. "We will move faster like this."

"Dude! Put me down! I don't know you!"

"You're about to spend the night naked with me. I think that me carrying you to expedite the process is within bounds, considering the circumstances."

I was quiet. He was right, and I had no right to protest the way that he wanted to touch my body. There didn't seem to be any jaguars hiding in this hidden maze of tunnels carved by secret rivers, and that was a huge plus in my book.

Up in front of us, I could see a glow of light. As we got closer, I could see that it was a small fire.

"Warm up. Take off your clothes."

I was a curvy girl. I knew that I already agreed. "Could you turn your back, please?"

"No. And my brother will not either." Out of the shadows, a guy walked out.

"Hello."

In the firelight, I could see both of their faces. "You guys are twins."

"It's common in our family, our Brood."

"Your Brood?"

"Our extended family, I guess you could say." He gestured toward the fire. "Take off your clothes. You should be clean." There was a water bucket next to the fire with a wet soapy cloth in it. "Wash yourself."

STRIPPING

I stripped off my clothes. I'd gotten pretty muddy while we walked through the network of caves, and I was glad that it wasn't going to dry on me. Mud is easy to take off when it is wet, but it is harder when you let it dry.

Both of the twins had a look on their faces like it was Christmas and I was what they'd asked Santa to bring them.

I picked up the soapy cloth. "Can you guys not stare?" I rubbed it on my arm.

"No," said the second twin bluntly. "Why would I ever look away? Your body is perfection."

"Even covered in mud?"

"I like the slide of the cloth over your body. When you are clean, I will clean you again with my tongue." His promise sent a shiver down my spine. I felt a lot like Little Red Riding Hood when the wolf was about to eat her up. Grandma, what big teeth you have.

"What are your names?"

"I am Dario," the first one said.

"Rico. And you?"

"Jade Esquibel." The two of them exchanged a glance. "How did you show up in the jungle right when my guide died?"

"That man was a fool to bring a young girl alone to the jungle. There are many things in the rain forest, and it's not safe for one such as you. You are defenseless."

"I am not!"

"I could master you in mere seconds, little girl."

I glared at him. "I might be short and curvy, but I'm not little."

"You are more 25 centimeters shorter than me."

I thought that was about 10 inches. "Yeah, so? It could just mean that you're gargantuan.

I startled laughs out of both of them. "We are many things, but we are not abnormally large. You have just incredibly small, my dear."

I finished cleaning the worst of the mud off. "Remember that when you eat me up."

Rico walked to me, and I realized that he was completely naked. He was fully erect, too. The firelight showed how many shadows his cock cast, and they were long. It wasn't my first time, but I was pretty sure that I couldn't fit that inside of my body. The last guy I'd been with was maybe half the girth. It was easy to get him in, but I hadn't felt much when he was inside of me. This cock was not a comfortable size, and I'd feel every inch of it stretching me past my limits.

"I have to taste you." He put a hand on my back and dipped me low in a movie-style kiss. I wrapped my arms around him just to keep my balance. If the whole night made me feel the fireworks I was feeling right now, then I'd consider the choice to spend the night with the two of them to be a good decision. It may even be the best decision of my life.

Rico abruptly straightened, and he pulled me up into his arms. I was impressed. I was not the tiniest of women, and he lifted me effortlessly.

"Don't drop me, please."

"I'd never drop you. You don't weigh anything." He walked out of the section that we were in, and we went to a huge bed with very dark purple sheets. I never knew that purple could be a masculine color, but the purple screamed "male" for some reason. He put me down, pushed me onto my back and began nuzzling my neck and breasts. His hot mouth on my breasts made me arch up into him.

Dario followed us into the room. He was naked, too, now. He wasn't as wide as his brother, but he was slightly longer. I could feel myself getting wet thinking about how he'd push into me and possess every inch of me. I thought that the bargain I had made to get out of the jaguar-infested rain forest was worth every moment that I would give them this night. Heck, I'd probably choose this if I had known what they were packing and there had been no jaguars.

"Brother, you can't have all of the fun." He climbed onto the bed and approached me on all fours. He captured my lips with his. It wasn't the kind of first kiss that said, "Hey, hi, how are you?" It was a kiss that said, "You should be mine for tonight, for tomorrow, and forever. You are mine." It was deeper and hotter than any kiss I'd had before, except for maybe Rico's.

Rico stopped suck and biting my breasts, and he kissed down the center of my body, including my soft tummy. He Frenched my belly button before sucking my clit into his mouth. I arched my back hard and moaned. It felt indescribable to feel his hot mouth on my body; I felt like there was lightning inside of me, and I didn't know if I could do from orgasmic pleasure. What a way to go, though.

Dario switched positions, too. He straddled my face. "Suck me."

I opened my mouth to let him thrust inside of my mouth. He pushed hard, and I had to try not to gag on his cock. He shot into my mouth, and I swallowed as much as I could. Meanwhile, Rico's tongue was pushing me higher and higher, and I squeezed my eyes shut as I soared and flew from his perfect mastery of my body.

When I opened my eyes again, Rico was pushing my legs as far apart as they would go. He had the cock head at my entrance, and he was teasing me with it slowly. I pushed my hips towards him, but he only pulled away.

"Beg."

"What?"

"Beg. If you want me, beg now."

"Please, please." I was far beyond caring about seeming uninterested. He had just given me an orgasm, but I needed more. I needed to feel him fill me up. I wanted Dario and Rico at the same time. I'd never done this before, but I was getting the hang of it pretty quickly. "Fuck me."

Rico slammed into me. He was too big, and I felt myself being torn apart. I'd never had anyone as big as him, and my body didn't know if I could take it. He didn't stop to let me get adjusted to his huge size, though. He set a demanding pace. With his hands on me, I couldn't move very much. I was pinned to the bed by his hips.

"Brother, I think it's time for a change in position. Let her ride you."

"Excellent idea." Rico rolled us over, and suddenly I could move on him. I was desperate for my next orgasm, and I pushed faster and faster to climb the peak. My knees were on either side of his body. His hands were on my hips, and he pulled me along quickly.

Dario put his hand on the back of my neck, and my torso lay flat on Rico's. I felt his hand reach between my thighs. My cum was all over the inside of my thighs, and he dragged it slowly back to my back door. I tensed up.

"Relax," Dario told me. "I am just readying you."

He pushed my ass checks apart, and he put his pinky inside of my ass. It was wet now, and I knew that it could take it. I'd never felt anything inside of my back door before, but it felt sinful and forbidden. It also was a tight fit, considering Rico's girth.

I kept pumping on him, and I could feel from the wilder bucks of Rico's hips that he was getting close to coming. I wouldn't give it to him, though. I wanted to ride him all night.

Dario was not going to wait all night, though. He pushed the tip of his dick at my ass. It was bigger than his pinky finger, and I was stretched already from Rico.

"I don't think it is going to fit."

"It will fit. You'll see. You were made for this. For us. For this moment." He pushed in a little further. I felt the stretch and the burn, but it felt so good. He pushed a little harder and faster, and I cried out. The intensity of everything was too much, with the rhythm that Rico was demanding from me and the feeling that Dario was evoking with his dick in my ass.

Dario snaked his hand around my front and started flicking my clit. I was a goner. I fluttered around the two of them, unable to control anything anymore. Rico shot first, but Dario was soon after him. I felt their seed fill me in both holes, and I felt it ooze out onto my thighs and the bed. We may have ruined the sheets, but the best sex of my life was worth it.

"That was so good." I was sticky now, after just having cleaned up, but I couldn't bring myself to care too much about it.

"Are you ready for more?" I could feel Dario's dick stir back to life inside of my ass.

"That's impossible. You can't be ready to go already! You just came twice."

"Baby, anything's possible with you. You are made for us. Mate us."

"Yes," I moaned. I was all for mating them up, down, and sideways.

Rico pulled my head down. He must have bitten his tongue a little when he came, because I could taste the slight taste of blood inside of his mouth. It also tasted like baklava, and it made me feel so warm to kiss him.

Dario began to slowly push in and out of my ass as his dick got back to full size. Rico's dick was still inside of me, and he was rapidly advancing towards full recovery, too, especially with the way we were making out.

This time, they were rougher. They knew I could take it, and the pace that they set for me was hard and fast. They shot a second time inside of me, and then I fell asleep, exhausted.

WAKING UP

When I woke up, the cave was still lit by firelight. The twins were beside me. I looked at their beautiful faces again. They were carved perfection. It was a shame that I had to leave after today, but I had a whole life to get back to. I was sure that the girls were going to get worried about me being gone. If Catie hadn't fallen asleep soon after dinner, then she had worried all night when I didn't come back from the nature hike.

"I know you're awake." Dario gently ran his hand over my curves. "Good morning."

"Good morning." I kissed him. "I wish I didn't have to go back. This night was like a perfect fantasy."

"What if you didn't? You were made for us, little Esquibel. Your family is a line of suitable mates. From the instant that we smelled you and saw you in our cave, we knew you were ours. Stay."

It was tempting. "I have responsibilities back home, you know. I have a family that would miss me. I can't just run off and have sex with two sexy twins all the time in the Amazon."

"What if I told you that all of your responsibilities would be fulfilled back home *and* you could have sex with two twins all the time in the Amazon? You are our mate, even if you don't understand it yet."

I didn't have to think about their offer. "I'd ask where I could sign up. Right now."

"I can make something. Be sure that this is your choice, though."

"What do you mean you can make something?"

All the talking woke Rico up. He began fingering my clit, which was very distracting.

"I can make a copy of you that will live your life, every moment of it, as if you were living it. It's a fairly simple piece of magic, although it takes quite a lot of energy to create and maintain."

"If that's true, I'll do it." I didn't want to torment myself, but this life was a much better one than the one that waited for me back in Middle America.

Dario flicked his hand. A carbon copy of me stood there. She was wearing the clothes that I had been wearing yesterday, only they weren't very dirty. She just looked tired.

"This is the you that they will find. She will live every second of your life."

Rico was bored with the conversation. He began laving me.

"Yes. Yes. I choose you." I bucked towards Rico's mouth. "I choose you."

I couldn't concentrate very well, but I watched my simulacrum walk out of the cave and head towards somewhere else. My old life walked out of that cave, and I was orgasmically happy with my new one.

EPILOGUE

*A*fter Dario and Rico mated me, I had to be presented to the queen. I had a virtually unlimited bank account, and I chose an evening gown to be presented to the queen. We took a flight all the way out to the Galapagos. The flight was long, and it was easier to just sit down for the whole thing.

When I got there, I got the surprise of my life. Alice was sitting on the throne.

"Hey girl!" Someone was calling me from behind. "How ya been?"

It was Gabriella. I gaped at her.

"You're dead."

"Nah, it was just my simulacrum. I think you know that now."

"Alice is here," I pointed at her sitting on the throne. "But Alice is back there, too."

"That's Alice's simulacrum. It lives her life exactly as she would have lived it. She dreams of her other life."

"So that's not weird, then, to dream about things that would happen if you were still at home?"

"No. It's the way that simulacra work. They pull extensively from you; they are you, just a parallel you."

"I'm glad to see that I'm not crazy." I rubbed an eyebrow. "I'd been having so many dreams about home, but I know that I'm not really home-sick. I'm happy with my mates." I looked Gabriella in the eye.

"I can see that Alice is the queen, and she has two consorts seated next to her. What are you doing here?"

Gabriella grinned. "I'm the Viceroy, sweetie. If you want to enter the crazy world of dragon politics, then you can go on and raise your hand.

CANOA

RAIN, RAIN

$\mathcal{I}$t was late and raining. I was tired. Lauren and I normally went for a run after conversation class, but the temperature and the rain combined were enough for us to call off our run.

"It's so gross." I peered out through the window, which was spattered with rain drops. Quito got a lot of rain.

"Yeah. I guess I'll see you tomorrow morning, then."

"You got it." I saluted her. "Do you want to catch the bus, or will you take a taxi home? Do you have an umbrella?"

"I have an umbrella. I'm just going to walk home. Got to save my money for the bars, haha."

"Ha. I'll see you tomorrow morning, then. Don't drink too much; you'll be dehydrated."

"Roger. See you." Lauren expanded her umbrella right as we got outside, and she walked north in the direction of her home. I watched her put on her hood, too; the wind wasn't too strong, but it made the rain smack you in the face.

I didn't live next to an Ecovia stop, so I had to either take a taxi or take a bus. I was too lazy to deal with the bus. The bus system in Quito is a little weird. It's completely run by private companies, so they go wherever, whenever. To someone used to the orderliness of the United States, it's a shock to find out that bus schedules do not exist. You just show up at a bus stop and hope that a bus swings by you. They have a list of destinations in the front window, and you pay them a set fee of twenty-five cents. In Quito, twenty-five cents is a lot of money. In America, I'd not feel an instant of guilt for not picking up a quarter that fell into a muddy puddle. Here, though, it represented much more spending power. We were more careful with our pennies, all of us, because people could and did use them, especially for public transport.

I went out the main street and hailed a taxi. I could have called Taxi Amigo from inside of the school building, but it was always really awkward to stand there next to the security guard. They were used to the American students who came in and out, but they only spoke Spanish. All of the students did, of course speak Spanish -- we couldn't be taking university courses in Spanish without it -- but it is one thing to read and write academic Spanish and another to converse in conversational Ecuadorian Spanish. So we kept to a smile and a wave most times.

The one time that I didn't, I had a really weird conversation with one of the new guards. There were two guards stationed there at the time, and one of them was an old hand. I waved to the new guard.

"Buenos dias."

"Buenos." He gave me a careful look. "How old are you?"

I was a little weirded out, but I shrugged. "Nineteen." I was almost 20.

"Do you have an older sister?"

"Yes, but she's in the United States." I waved goodbye, and I went to the elevators.

Later, the other security guard had apologized for the new guy's behavior. He evidently didn't believe that it was professional to try to flirt with teenage college students. I shrugged it off, though. Ever since I hit puberty, I'd gotten attention like that.

I wasn't anything special. I had a runner's body, true, with the big runner's thighs and ripped calves that came with it. I had a pretty muscular ass, if I did say so myself, and I had boobs that constantly got in the way as a runner. I had sports bras that could hold watermelons, and they were the only thing that kept the girls safe. I felt like they were a curse as a runner, but my mother told me that I'd be glad to have them one day.

So far, the only thing that they'd gotten me was a lot of unwanted male attention. I didn't date much; going out and partying with frat boys wasn't my style in college. I played video games sometimes, and I was most likely to be found at the gym, taking some kind of class. I'd tried a lot of different things: Zumba, cardio kickboxing, and yoga. My favorite was kickboxing, because we had real punching bags. It was self-defense class coupled with cardio. I had to learn the forms, but it was a lot of fun to do. It made me feel like such a badass.

In Quito, my fitness time had been channeled into a lot of running with Lauren. Professional athletes train at high altitudes. At first, I'd been embarrassingly breathless and wheezed like an overweight dog. But, as time went on, I got better. I wasn't as good as Lauren, who had won a marathon in Quito, but I was good enough to keep up with her sometimes. The running that she did with me was all about endurance, not about speed. She did sprints and stuff on her own. I was more of a long-distance runner, and I wasn't as competitive as she was about it. How much she drank was surprising to me, but that was ok. I mean, I'm not really one to judge. I went through an extremely crazy phase during freshman year, but I'd sobered up when it had impacted my grades.

I was from an Irish Catholic family, and my mom didn't touch a drop of alcohol. She had seen it mess up their family, and I had a late great-uncle who had been something of an alcoholic. I didn't blame them, much, but I'd spent a lot of time doing extracurriculars in high school -- cross country, choir, and track -- so I hadn't had a lot of time to party. I was not a cheer-leader kind of girl anyway. So, I went to one party in high school, saw everyone toking up and drinking their parents' booze, and swore off of the teen scene altogether. Getting caught was not worth the risk. I had scholar-ships and stuff on the line from my running.

I got plantar fasciitis my freshman year, which was rotten luck. In order to keep my scholarship, I worked as the student manager of the cross country team. It was not the same thing as running with all of them, but it helped keep the toll off of my body. In order to rehabilitate my feet, I'd gone to a podiatrist, who gave me orthotics and prednisone. I also went to a chiro-practor, who did all kinds of weird things not only with my feet but with my Achilles tendon and stuff, too. My plantar fasciitis now was mostly gone, but I knew that it was considered a chronic condition. I wasn't ready to go full-tilt back into competitive running.

I ran for myself, nowadays. In Quito, I ran with Lauren around La Carolina and sometimes other parks when we wanted to switch it up. La Carolina was very convenient, since it was right next to school, though. We had so much fun running through. We were a striking pair, Lauren and I, with her white-blonde Nordic hair and my flame-red Irish hair. My mom's family was from Southern Ireland, which meant that we were Black Irish. Everyone else in my family ended up with dark hair, but I had the flame-red hair of my grandmother. We joked sometimes that I was the red-headed stepchild. It was a joke, but it was true, too. Nobody else in my family was athletic in the same way that I was; I was lucky that my mom considered it healthy that I ran so much, and she completely financially supported all sports-related endeavors as I grew up.

In college, I'd had to cover my own things. So the manager job paid a little bit, and I had scholarships for tuition, fees, room, and board. What I really needed money for was all the extra stuff, like going to restaurants or buying extra groceries to eat something that wasn't cafeteria food. I had some money saved up and inherited, but I preferred to have cash flow instead of spending down my savings. As a result, I freelanced as a graphic designer on elance. it didn't bring in much money, but I liked being able to design things for people. I'd grown up pretty artistic, but I'd never fit in with the artsy kids. I wasn't dark enough for them. In high school, I'd taken one drawing class, and I'd been on my own the whole time. It was the end of my artistic career at the time. College was more freeing, and I was getting a bachelor of fine arts. My second major was computer science. Because I was out of high school, I was able to do a lot of things that wouldn't have been socially allowed. I hung out with the art kids, the compsci nerds for gaming nights, and with the runners that I managed. It was a disparate set of groups, but I loved them all in their own ways.

That was really why I felt comfortable being friends with Lauren and with the other group. There was one group that I could sit down with and pound out anthropology essays with the night before they were due. Lauren's group was the kind that was phenomenally fun to go to salsa dancing with. They all took salsa classes, and I went with them for it. It was fun, and it was a different way of moving than the small amount of ball-room dancing I was exposed to in cotillion class in the United States. They were groups of friends who satisfied different needs. We went to Seseribo at least once a week, and that was a very fun experience. There were professional dancers there, who were perfect and beautiful to watch. Then, there was us. The other girls got asked out by Ecuadorians, and I was the one left to watch all of our coats at the table. I didn't mind, though. Sitting back at the table was enough for me; trying to deal with a handsy Ecuadorian guy who wanted to touch you under the guise of "dancing" wasn't my speed.

I hung out with Lauren less than she would have liked. We were the closest people to each other, and we got each other the best. However, her social life and mine didn't overlap too much. I was much happier making a spaghetti dinner with the other girls than going to a club. Once, we'd made garlic bread. When we took it out of the oven, the bread was blue-green on top. It was the weirdest thing. We didn't know if it was safe to eat, but frankly in Ecuador, we leapt way before we looked. We ate it anyway, and none of us got indigestion, so that was good.

It was more restful to go to trivia nights and stay in than it was to go out and party as hard as possible with Ecuadorian guys. I was a pretty good kid at home, and after I'd shaken out the kinks my freshman year, I went back to being the good kid who stayed home most nights. My parents would have been proud, if they had any idea of what I did or didn't do at night.

The taxi brought me home, and I waved to the doorman as I came in. He nodded at me. I was so visibly American -- flame-red hair and freckled, pale skin -- that he knew that I wasn't Ecuadorian. It was fine. He was courteous, and that's all that I needed.

HOME

I walked up the stairs to my apartment on the third floor. It was dark. My parents weren't home yet. They'd bring home take-out, and it would be a quiet meal. They worked a lot. I was really ok with it, though. My host family wasn't true family to me, and I kept quiet inside. They didn't mind it when I went out with my friends, and I barely told them beforehand. I did tell them before they left work, though, so that they knew that picking up take-out for me wasn't important. I was happier eating some paella with my friends than I was eating some pseudo-American fast food from an Ecuadorian joint.

I started doing my homework, which wasn't too bad. I had to read two different studies for my anthropology class. I opened up a Spanish dictionary on my computer. I was good enough at Spanish, but taking university classes in Spanish was a whole other level. I needed to be able to look up any words that I'd never heard in English. This anthropology class was my first one, and it was likely to be my last. I had too much stuff to fit into college; this semester was really my wild one, because I had a pretty rigidly defined set of courses for the rest of my college career back home. Computer science was no joke as a degree, and my BFA was demanding in its own way, too. Therefore, this sojourn in Ecuador was my idea of breaking free. No one had to know what I did or didn't take; I was filling out the Spanish minor that I needed for my computer science major, and that was satisfactory degree progress for my advisors in the School of Informatics and School of Arts and Sciences. When it came down to it, they were really there to make sure that you were playing the right game. If I had been a different sort of girl, then it would've been harder to get advisor approval for doubling up in two very demanding majors. I didn't mind it though.

Nobody in Ecuador knew what my main majors were. We all just assumed that everyone was some kind of Spanish major and left it there. I found the less that I talked about my life back home, the less anyone was interested in what I was doing. I liked it that way. I'm private, and I felt like I'd fit in better without saying anything.

It meant that some of my nerdier aspects were hidden. One of my side projects was setting up an Android game from scratch. None of my classes so far had taught me mobile game development; the school, unlike cooler ones, did not even offer it. I'd taught myself using a Udacity course, and I had a nanodegree in Android app development. I could never hope to get to the incredible heights of Flappy Bird, but making the game itself was soothing to me. Because of my art degree, I was unusually good at user experience stuff. My side design work had honed my skills enough for me to be able to wireframe and then code pretty awesome games.

I'd seen a trickle of money with my very first game. Thank goodness that Google Play let in a lot more apps than the iStore did. It was true that the iStore paid out a lot more to developers, but you went through an incredible amount of hassle in order to get your apps in front of paying customers. The time that you had to spend to resolve the issues that they nitpicked was better spent making a new game, in my opinion. I wasn't bad at debugging, and I wasn't likely to push a game that wasn't ready into the store, but I also wasn't just going to spend all of my time looking at old code when I could be writing new code.

My desperate wish of my heart was to earn enough money as a one-woman shop that I wouldn't have to find a job when I was ready to graduate. My mom had already been pushing me to get an internship for this summer, and there were a lot of places that really wanted to get more females in there. I didn't know, though. The game industry was pretty male-dominated, and I would much rather code from home and go by an a gender-neutral pen name on the boards.

If I did get a real job, I'd probably specialize in mobile user experience. I understood it, and I was weirdly in love with the world of UX. I had a cousin who was a UX guy for EREcnc, and he had made some solid bank from his equity compensation. He was still weirdly, working though. I'd asked him about.

"Why the hell are you still working? Shouldn't you be living on a beach in Cabo or something?"

He laughed. "How much money do you think I have?"

"A lot. Your company is in the billion-dollar valuation club."

He shook his head. "It's all on paper. If the company tanked -- and it could at any minute -- I'd be left with a double handful of nothing, unable to pay the mort-

gage on my Cabo getaway." He ruffled my hair. *"I'm pretty happy making cash, Fitz."*

"If I were you, I'd sell my shares on the second market, travel, and then come back and start my own business."

"Well, if you want to, I'll give you some startup capital when you want it. That's a promise."

I actually had some money from our grandmother, who died early in the fall semester of my sophomore year. We both did, and it was enough to buy a new car. It wasn't going to launch me into the stratosphere, but it was enough to make me feel safe. I worked for my extra money, because it was a habit that I'd picked up my freshman year. I wanted to be a normal college student as much as possible, and I figured that the work experience was being paid to learn new things. Learning was worth more than the money.

My grandmother's money was sitting quietly in some index funds. I wasn't savvy enough to figure out how to invest it as a teenager, and I'd gone with the simple, easy way of dealing with it. It seemed simple enough to diversify with the stocks of zillions of different companies. Even if one fell, not all of them would.

I'd gotten a surprising amount of return on a very boring, not risky investment. It was honestly enough for me to not work to supplement for the extras, but it was not enough for me to feel safe just throwing caution to the wind. Just barely enough money didn't make me feel safe at all.

In Ecuador, our trips were funded with that investment income. I still picked up some design jobs. I had less stuff to do here, which meant that my portfolio was growing slowly. I got some good reviews from the people that I'd worked with, and the portfolio spoke for itself. I'd been jacking up my rates by about 10% every job. And I knew that at some point, I'd hit the top of what people were willing to pay. I hadn't found it yet, though. I was fine with that. Some day, I'd make a lot doing UX, either for me or other people.

I researched venture capitalists with single-minded intensity. I listened to what they said about "marketing" and "distribution" being the hottest words. I knew that they didn't want to stare at wireframes during a pitch meeting, and they wanted an MVP before any kind of pitch. I knew that they didn't want Power Points, because they had to stare at them all day. They wanted multimedia presentations, including user testimonials especially.

There's a saying in the car industry about selling cars. "Touch it; feel it." That applied during investor meetings, too. They wanted to be able to use it, and they wanted it to be very easy to use. That's why my UX experience was so important; I might end up as a technical co-founder, and I was confident in my ability to be a product person.

Because I was getting ready to build my own business, I was also getting a certificate in business. I really wanted to just learn the basics of how to run a business, and it was nice to meet the business kids, too. I was doing a lot in college, but I figured that it was an all-you-can-eat buffet of knowledge. I was be a complete fool not to gorge myself on the knowledge of the ages. The professors I had were experts in their fields, and they knew more about their fields than they could possibly teach me. I loved learning hard, and I didn't resent doing homework out of the textbook or anything.

I tried really hard to fit in with my host family. So, when I got home and got out of the taxi, I gave my host mother an Ecuadorian-style hug and kiss on the cheek.

"How was your day?"

"It was ok. How was yours?"

"Good, good. We got some new clients today, so I had to do a lot more than usual. Busy. It was good. Do you want a smoothie?"

"Yes, I'd love one."

I sat down with her in our breakfast nook in the kitchen. She poured me a glass, and I took a sip. The cold smoothie tasted sweet and fruity. It slid smoothly down my throat.

"Do you have a boyfriend?"

I choked a little bit. "Um, no. Why?"

"Oh, I was just curious. Every girl has a boyfriend."

Let's see. I had a friend with extremely restricted benefits. We made out and cuddled whenever he could convince me to come over. That wasn't really a boyfriend to me; he didn't require the relationship maintenance that other people would, and I didn't feel as strongly about him as I wanted to feel about my first real boyfriend. So, no, I didn't have a boyfriend.

"I don't," I reassured her. I drained my glass. "I'm going to go do my homework now."

"Ok, good luck. Study hard!"

I smiled back at her, and then I escaped into my bedroom so that I could get some work done.

FACEBOOK GROUP MESSAGES

J wouldn't be a college student without procrastinating, though. I went to Facebook first, and I saw that I had a message from Lauren. It was a group message.

Hey girls!

Let's party this weekend in Canoa! I heard that it's populated with hot surfers. It's just one bus transfer at night, and then we'll be there in the morning.

The rest of the thread was all the blonde bar flies agreeing to go. If I went, then I'd stick out like a sore thumb whenever they went to bars. I didn't drink much.

I was such a closet nerd. I felt like people couldn't see me for me, but that was me, not them. I was incredibly private. I sometimes was told that I was snobby, but I didn't think that it was accurate. I was just a little bit shy.

Coming to Ecuador had changed that. Lauren had changed it most of all. She had such a take-charge attitude, like the entire world should bow before her. I wasn't like that, but she made it seem easy and simple to be someone I had never been before. She took it as her due that she would have the best of all the friends, and somehow I got caught up in that. I guess it was running, though I was not really sure what she saw in me when all of her other friends were tall blondes with Daddy's credit card. I was a ginger who was just making my way.

I was a different version of myself here, that was sure, but it was a better version. I'd be integrating some of who I was back into my old life, because it was a stronger, better version of me. It was like I had unveiled the Fitz that had always been inside of me. Lauren made me strong, even though I wasn't exactly like her.

I didn't have any friends like her in the United States. Her strong personality honestly probably would have had me running away screaming. But in this country, we only had each other, and that was what tossed us together multiple times a day.

Lauren was beautiful, with hair that was white-blond and eyes that were blue as the sky. She'd never known for a day in her life what it was like not to have the world bow at her feet. There was a self-possession and a pure confidence that came with never, ever being denied.

She'd grown up with a doting father who loved his little angel and a mother who thought that she was a doll. She could have ended up as a coddled little princess, unable to handle the world. Instead, she'd grown up into a Valkyrie. She was like Veruca Salt without the pure rottenness that went all the way through her. Lauren was a good person.

I didn't have the same kind of background, but a handful of my friends (I'd only had a handful of friends) had doting parents like that. One of the runners on the team had a cocaine addiction. She bought really great clothes, and her parents -- her divorced mom and dad -- didn't think that it was weird that she asked for money constantly. She bought enough clothing with her cash that they didn't think that it was weird. It was a sad thing, I thought, but I shut up. My schoolmates didn't like narcs. I didn't try too much to fit in, but I didn't do too much to stand out, either.

I added to the thread something that might mitigate my misery.

Hey, can I bring other friends along?

Lauren replied immediately.

Yeah! The more, the merrier.

I sent a text to all my other girls, the ones who would feel comfortable with me drinking nonalcoholic beverages.

Hey guys! Do you want to go to the beach this weekend? Lauren and some others are hitting Canoa.

I got some texts from Alice, Catie, and Jade immediately. They were all in.

BUS DEPOT

*L*ate on Thursday night, all of us met at the bus depot station. It wasn't Quitumbe or La Ofelia; it was the parking lot that the bus company owned. It was dark, and it felt shady. I was glad that I was with so many other girls and not on my own. All of us bought tickets at their ticket counter.

We brought all of our stuff inside of the bus with us. I hoped it wouldn't be too crowded. Nobody seemed to want to leave their stuff in the compartments under the bus; at night, it was too easy for someone to get on and off the bus with our stuff. It was better to leave the straps connected to our wrists or ankles. In the bus from Ingapirca to Cuenca, someone, an Ecuadorian stranger, had gotten their stuff sorta stolen. She'd had the strap around her ankle, and she was sleeping. Two shady guys cut her purse open by crouching on the floor and reaching under the seat. Someone had noticed, and she'd woken up. There had been an incredible ruckus, and the two guys immediately got off the bus.

I was relieved, but one of the Ecuadorians chewed out the bus driver.

You shouldn't have let them off. You should've taken them to the police.

What do I look like, a hero? I am just a bus driver. What if they had a knife? What if they had guns? We are better off without them here.

I agreed with that sentiment. In America, those guys would've been taken to justice for sure. Here, in the other America, the justice system was a little bit broken.

Another thing that killed me about traveling in Ecuador was the lack of bathrooms. I'd been on long bus rides for field trips in school, and there was always a gross-smelling bathroom at the back that reeked of chemicals. I didn't understand how necessary that was until I got to Ecuador. In Ecuador, none of the buses had bathrooms in them. You just held it for a 10-hour bus ride. There were no rest stops. They only stopped for long enough to take on new passengers and let the old ones go. I considered it lucky that they fully stopped, unlike the Quito buses.

Some of us carried empty plastic bottles for that purpose, but it seemed really gross to me to carry around your urine. So, I made sure not to drink anything or eat any soup the day before. Mild dehydration was a better deal for me than carrying around a warm bottle of my pee. I could always drink more when we got to our destination.

I wished that we were flying instead. It was cheap to fly in Ecuador, much cheaper than flying around inside of the US. A flight on Southwest that went one-way cost around $70 if you took the cheapest route.

In Ecuador, a round-trip flight cost $70, especially if you got it during an LAN sale. I loved how much faster planes were than buses. However, buses went straight to more places, and you knew exactly where you'd end up when you left Quito. We used buses for every trip except the one to Cuenca, which would've been a bus ride exceeding 10 hours over and around the Andes.

I tried to sleep for as much of the bus ride as possible. There was a huge gossiping session going on between the blondes about Ecuadorian guys, but Alice and Jade were already dozing. Catie had brought her ever-faithful companions, our books for Andean literature class. She was already gearing up for our final term paper, which was a cross-book literary analysis. The four of us were pretty good kids, but Catie definitely took the cake with how earnest she was.

In elementary school, all of us were required to have an assignment note-book. In every subject, we had things for homework. I'd stopped using an assignment notebook sometime in college, but Catie became that assignment notebook for me in Ecuador. We had every class together, and she knew exactly what was happening when. I permanently co-opted her for study sessions, and she led them at her house. We'd bake cookies or cook real food, and all of us would study together for our upcoming exams. It wasn't a bad system. Catie was always ahead of the game.

I blocked out the chatter behind me, closed my eyes, and fell asleep.

CATIE SHOOK ME. I woke up. The hum of the motor was quiet, and it was dark outside. "Girl, we're in Rocafuerte. We have to transfer here."

"Ok." I was still pretty groggy. I got my backpack, and I walked out of the bus. There were painted benches in the bus station. The bus schedule on the wall showed that the connecting bus to Canoa would be there in two hours. I laid down on my backpack and went back to sleep.

∼

Catie shook me awake again. "Wake up! The next bus is here. Get out your boleto."

I sat up. I could feel a zipper imprint on my cheek, and I put my hand to my cheek. Yup, I had zigzags from using my backpack as a pillow. I rubbed my eyes, and I got on my feet. I dug into my jacket pocket to take out my boleto, so that I could show my ticket to the bus driver as we got on the bus that would take us the rest of the way to Canoa.

Dawn was breaking at this point, and the pink fingers stretched everywhere. It would have been more beautiful if I hadn't been so tired. I stayed awake. There was no point in going back to sleep, because the rest of the trip was less than the time that we'd waited in Rocafuerte.

I stared at the lush Pacific coast greenery that lined the road. The coast looked a lot different from the Andes, especially the civilized Quito where I lived. There were a lot more palm trees, for one thing, and far fewer buildings. Wild bananas were everywhere.

At the bus station, there were a lot of weird taxis. I guessed they would be called rickshaws, if you were being technical about it. All of them were glad to pick up a large group of American girls, and they took us straight to a hostel. They must have had a kickback system with the owner. I got off, and I touched Lauren's shoulder.

"Are you sure you want to go to this hotel? It seems sketchy that we went here straight first thing. Don't you want —"

"Fitz, I get that, but I'm tired. I don't want to walk to the hotel next door. I'd rather just lay down right now."

I shrugged. "Ok."

We let Alice take the lead when it came to talking to the natives. Her internal calculator was a lot better than anything I could do, and she could negotiate in Spanish better than a native Ecuadorian could. She managed to knock 20% off of the list price for the sake of all of us staying in their hostel. It wasn't a small amount of money with how many of us there were. Because she had negotiated it so low, they made us pay in cash beforehand, instead of paying on checkout like you would at an American hotel.

All of us took out our wallets and paid for our rooms in cash. With our lighter pockets, we all walked upstairs. The four of us were in one place, and Lauren and the others took another large room across the hall. We all went back to sleep.

FOOD AND BEACH

*A*round 10 AM, I woke up. I could see Catie sitting on her bed and reading. When she heard me get out of bed and stand up, she looked up.

"Hey!"

"Hey, Catie."

"Do you want to grab breakfast? I'm kinda starving."

"That sounds good." My stomach rumbled. "It looks like I'm hungry, too."

I grabbed my wallet and phone, just in case the other girls woke up while we were out, and we walked out.

Downstairs, they had a bunch of people eating at their bar. I snagged a menu from the side. The prices were gringo prices, and there wasn't that much variety.

"Let's go somewhere else," I said to Catie. "The prices are too high, and I'd rather have something besides fish."

"Ugh, fish," Catie wailed. "Ok, I'm ready to walk somewhere else."

We walked into town, and we went straight to a bakery. Our noses led us to the fresh bread. They had all kinds of food. They had little fruit tarts, croissants, normal bread, French bread, and these fruit empanadas filled with oranges, bananas, and other kinds of fruit.

Catie and I bought a couple of the little things a piece. I also bought two loaves of French bread for the rest of the girls. I knew that all of us were going to be starving when we woke up.

We took our haul back to our hostel, and Catie and I ate our breakfasts.

The noise that we made when we came back up the metal stairs woke everyone up. Lauren and the other girls came into our room, and we all ate a little of the bakery stuff.

"Do you guys want to get lunch?"

"That sounds good. I need to brush my teeth, but after that we should get something."

All of us scrambled to wash up, because the bread hadn't done much to fill our stomachs up.

When we were all dressed and ready, we walked down to a restaurant. We chose one that was just a block away from the hotel. It had a limited prix-fixe menu, but that was fine with me. I had never seen so many prix-fixe restaurants before, but it was how they did things in Ecuador.

We sat down, and all of us ordered freshly squeezed juice. Tropical fruit was abundant here; it was basically falling off the trees. Unlike the Midwest, where I am from, Ecuador grows everything year-round, it seemed. Sure, there are two seasons, rainy and sort of dry, but it was hot enough for people to grow crops all the time.

Fruit fell off the trees. There were real orchards, of course, but there were many wild fruit trees, too. You could pick up a lime from a tree without any hassle. Back home, that cost around 25 cents at the grocery store. Here, it was free. When we had told our Ecuadorian friends that we'd paid 25 cents for a lime or lemon at home, they thought it was ridiculous. You just get it off of the tree, they told us.

It was a different world, and it was definitely a different culture. We had our soup course first, then some fish (which Catie shoved onto Alice's plate) and bananas, and then some more fruit for postre. I was glad that I'd eaten breakfast less than two hours ago, because the Ecuadorian portion sizes -- the kind that they gave American girls, anyway -- were not enough for a steady runner like me.

When we were done and paid for the meal, Lauren stood up. "Let's go to the beach, guys."

We all went to our rooms and changed into our swimsuits. We put on sunglasses. With all of us carrying our beach towels, we made our way to the beach. It wasn't very far from the hostel.

All of us got busy smearing sunscreen on each others' backs. It had been weird earlier in the semester -- someone touching your bare back is actually a pretty intimate thing -- but it had quickly been overcome, like our American sensibilities about undressing around each other. I had no problem with it, having spent so much time in locker rooms, but the other girls had taken time to get used to it.

All of us just laid out. There were creepy Ecuadorian men taking pictures of all of us in our bikinis, but we ignored them, until Lauren started getting into their faces. They left after that. Alice ran into the ocean. I didn't think that it was a good idea so close to lunch, but I was her friend, not her mother.

Catie had brought her book in her bag, and she was reading Pedro Paramo again. I turned on my back so that the sun could hit my back, and I fell asleep with a full stomach.

LAS CUCARACHAS

Catie woke me up when everyone was ready to go back. I felt kinda thirsty, and I made a mental note to drink more water. Restricting my water intake before and then not refilling as soon as I got to Canoa was a mistake. It was good that Lauren and I weren't foolish enough to go running in an unknown place, because it probably would have been a problem for me. It would be easier to breathe here, though, at sea level. Swimming was enough exercise for me, and it didn't carry the risk of aggravating my plantar fasciitis.

We headed up to get changed, and we rinsed off the sand. I had one of those cool convertible bikini sets that could double as underwear, which cut down on how much I had to pack. It would have been awful to stick around in wet underthings, but they were quick dry, and I was fully dry before the other girls were done. I put back on my clothes then. We went to the same restaurant for dinner; the service was ok, and the prices were good.

After filling our stomachs with soup, fish, and fruit, Lauren and the others were ready to hit the bars and clubs. Alice, Catie, and Jade were less keen on going there, so I took them back to the hostel. Alice dropped off immediately, and Catie and Jade weren't far behind. I was the only one awake when the cockroaches came.

WITH HORROR, I watched them climb all over my backpack and everyone else's. I didn't want to wake up everyone else by screaming, but I ran down the metal staircase as fast as I could. I went to the desk.

"There are cockroaches!"

"Is that so?"

"Can you get rid of them?"

The guy at the desk sighed. "Of course." He rummaged around under the desk and brought out a fumigator. He climbed the staircase before me. When he got into our room, he didn't wake up anyone or anything. He just started spraying all of the walls. The fumes were definitely not healthy, and in America, we evacuated people before we sprayed dangerous chemicals.

My backpack was now covered in cockroach-killing spray. He left.

I woke all the others. "Guys! Guys. There are cockroaches."

Alice sat up. "Cockroaches!" She tucked her feet under her. "Where?" She looked around.

"Well, the guy got rid of them with some spray, but I don't feel safe staying here. What if they come back?"

"Ew," Jade murmured quietly.

"I'm tired," Catie said.

"So am I," chimed the other two.

"We've already paid for the entire weekend," Alice pointed out sensibly. "It's late."

"Guys, I'm not staying here. There were cockroaches in my stuff!" They didn't care. "I'm going to go to the hostel next door. I'll meet you guys for breakfast tomorrow." I held up my cell phone in my right hand. "I'll have my phone."

"Sounds good." Catie covered her mouth with her left hand to mask a yawn. "I'll see you tomorrow."

HOTEL

$\mathcal{N}$ext door to our hostel was a fancier place, which was an actual hotel. It also had a fancy price, but it was worth it if it meant that I wouldn't have cockroaches in my backpack. I checked in right behind two guys wearing suits.

In America, that would have meant that they were at work. In Ecuador, that was part for the course with the middle class. In a highly stratified society, class mattered. When you wore a suit, it meant that you could afford to hire someone to custom tailor a suit for you. It was so cheap here to get a custom-made suit that I bought 5. They would come in handy some day, and the cost of custom-made suits was cheaper than just an off-the-rack suit jacket back home.

It was cheap to live the life of the hoi aristoi here, because labor was cheap. With a lack of employment opportunities, there were a lot of people who did things called subempleo, like selling lottery tickets on street corners or gum in La Mariscal. People did what they had to get by, just as they did in every country in the world.

I wasn't particularly impressed by the super slick guys, although they were definitely way taller than most Ecuadorian guys. They were pale, too, with no Latin blood. Either they were not from here, or they were German.

When they were done, I walked up to the front. "I'd like a room tonight, please."

"Certainly. How many people?"

"Just me."

"Ok. A single costs $100 a night."

That was pretty steep for Ecuador, but it still beat sleeping with cockroaches crawling all over me. "Ok."

The key that they gave me took me to the top floor. It was split into two different penthouses. I had an amazing view over the water. I suspected that the desk receptionist had given me the most expensive room because I was American and theoretically able to afford it. I didn't splash money around like this, but it was worth it for one night. I'd spend $100 on a hotel room in the United States, and peace of mind was worth more than the money that I was spending on this room.

I'd be eating empanadas tomorrow, as we left, because I'd just drained almost all of my cash with this room, unless I found an ATM and paid the international fee for withdrawal.

I was getting undressed when I heard a knock on my door. Maybe the desk receptionist was going to give me toothpaste.

"Coming!" I called. I put my clothes back on quickly. I opened the door.

It wasn't the desk receptionist. It was one of the two guys in suits.

"Hello."

"Goodbye," I said. "What are you doing here?" I took in a deep breath to scream.

"Shh," the other one said. "We're not here to hurt you." He brandished a bottle of wine at me. "We were going to invite you to join us."

I relaxed a little.

"Sorry about that," he said, not sounding sorry at all. "I didn't want you wake everyone else up. The penthouses are soundproofed anyway."

I walked away to put some distance between me and the first guy. "Who are you, and why are you in my room?"

"Allow us to introduce ourselves. I am Edmundo."

"And I am Ramiro."

"Tell me, my dear. What is your name?"

"Amelia Fitzwilliam Bello. Everyone calls me Fitz, though."

"Well, Ms. Fitz Bello, we are pleased to make your acquaintance."

"Why are you in my room?"

Edmundo and Ramiro exchanged a look. "Why don't we tell you a little about ourselves first?"

"Fair enough."

"We're businessmen, and we're based in Canoa. Well, our business interests are a little outside of here, but close enough. When we saw you downstairs, we thought that you were a very pretty girl."

Ok, that was moderately flattering, but it still didn't excuse them for breaking into my room and stopping me from screaming. If their intentions were honorable, they wouldn't have minded other people coming in. "Tell me why I shouldn't kick you guys out and call the desk receptionist?"

"We hope that there is as reason that you could, ahem, stay in Canoa."

"Why on earth would I stay in Canoa?" I asked. "There's nothing for me here."

"Would you like a drink?" He uncorked the bottle by tapping the bottom.

"Sure." He poured me some wine into a dark glass which made the wine seem darker, and it was fizzy and good. The bottle's label said Dom Perignon. They drank, too.

"Do you ever wonder what life would be like if you didn't live a mundane life?"

That was a jump in conversation. "I'm a little young for my quarter-life crisis, thanks."

"Do you?"

"I mean, I guess. I'm pretty happy with the way that things are, though."

Edmundo crossed the room to look out the window. "Would you like to see something magical? We'll be in public, I promise."

"Ok."

"Do you have a swimming suit? Unless you wish to go skinny dipping, that would be advisable."

"I actually have it on right now."

"Ok." Edmundo led the way out of our hotel.

SEX ON THE BEACH

*J*t was dark outside, and there was nobody on the beach but us. There were lights, though, and they reassured me. I wasn't about to be lost forever in the ocean.

The water was breathtaking. There were zillions of tiny points of light in there.

"What are the glowing things? Is it safe to go in the water? It looks radioactive. Will it give me superpowers like Spiderman?"

They both laughed.

"No," Edmundo reassured me. "No, you won't get any superpowers from them. They are green phosphorescent bacteria. It is beautiful, yes?"

"Yeah, it's great." I stripped down to my swimsuit, and I ran into the surf. A million little lights swirled around me.

The boys were close behind me. They shed their suits in no time, heedless of how sandy they would get on the bare beach. They came towards me in just their underwear, and we started a splash fight. It was fun -- the kind of good, clean, coed fun that I hadn't had since I came to Ecuador. It was isolating to only be in a group of girls. Lauren and company mitigated that by seeking the company of Ecuadorian men, and I was finding out why. It was fun. They were fun.

I felt like a constellation, because I was covered in tiny stars.

They stopped splashing me, and they moved in closer. Edmundo reached in. He put his forehead on mine.

"You are so beautiful, corazon." He captured my lips in a gentle kiss, and he reached his huge hands around my waist. Ramiro was behind me, and he pushed his powerful erection in my ass. I could feel myself getting really wet in a way that had nothing to do with standing in the ocean. Ramiro's hands were inside of the front of my bikini bottoms, and he was playing with my clit.

My nipples were hard enough to cut through diamond. Edmundo gently tilted my head back by pulling on my hair, and he kissed my throat and the tops of my breasts. He pulled down my bikini top so that he could suckle on my nipples and bite my breasts. I felt like I was burning up inside; my bones were jelly. Each kiss turned me on more, and my knees were feeling weak.

Ramiro was pulling down my bottoms now, and I didn't care that we were on a public beach where anyone could see us. I cared more about being skin-to-skin with Ramiro. I couldn't wait to feel his cock thrust inside of me.

He pushed his dick between my muscled thighs, and he pushed forward. He wasn't inside of me; we were just having intercrural sex. I was wet with my juices and the ocean water. His dick was really long, and I could see the tip peek out from between my legs. He put his hand back on my clit, with one on my hip as he thrust forward, and I couldn't see anymore.

Edmundo's hands came down to my ass, and he hauled me up so that my legs were wrapped around him. It gave Ramiro the access he needed to plunge into me. He wasn't slow about it. He thrust into me sharply, in one thrust. He sheathed himself entirely inside of my body.

I cried out. I'd never had sex in public before, but the thrill of maybe being discovered made me even wetter. If they couldn't see us, they would definitely hear us.

Edmundo thrust his tongue into my mouth, and he tongue-fucked me as Ramiro pumped again and again into my body. My arms were around his neck, and I was holding on for dear life. Ramiro didn't let me do any of the work; it was all him, pushing me harder into the rock-solid body of his brother.

"Brother," Ramiro panted. "I think that you should feel her."

For some reason, that made sense to Edmundo, because he nodded. Ramiro pulled out of me, and I felt so empty without him inside of me.

Not for long. He pushed his fingers into my pussy, and then he took my wetness to the back door. I stiffened up, and I stopped kissing Edmundo.

"Wait."

Ramiro kissed the back of my neck. "Sh, little one. It will feel good, I promise."

I loosened up a little bit, and he pushed past my tight sphincter. It felt incredible to be stretched there, even though it burned.

Edmundo was holding me with one hand now, and he stationed himself at my pussy. I could feel his hard tip impatiently waiting.

Ramiro evidently felt that I was stretched and ready enough, because he pushed his gigantic cock into my ass.

"Ah!" It was so big. I put my face on Edmundo's shoulder.

"Breathe." Ramiro kissed my shoulder, and it made me loosen. "Breathe." He pushed in and out again.

Edmundo wasn't waiting any longer. He thrust into my already-sore pussy, and he took me in powerful strokes. Ramiro and Edmundo timed each stroke perfectly. There was some pain, yes, but there was indescribable pleasure from being filled with two cocks. Edmundo was still expertly kissing me, though the kiss was savage. I'd never been kissed by anyone as if they were a dying man and I was an oasis in the desert.

Ramiro was the first to climax, bellowing loudly. I felt him shoot into my ass, and I felt it drip out. The sensation pushed me over the edge, and I screamed as I climaxed. Edmundo grabbed my hips hard enough to leave bruises with both hands, and he thrust without any rhythm, just animal savagery. He pushed deeper into me than I'd ever had any man before.

I didn't know that I could climax so quickly twice in a row, but I was learning right now. I pushed against Edmundo, and the stimulation was enough to tip me over the edge. I cried out again, and the contractions of my muscles must have pushed Edmundo to the brink, too. He roared as he pushed into me and shot everything into my womb.

I fought to catch my breath. Edmundo put me back on my feet again, and I let the ocean cleanse me of all the juices running out of me. My bikini bottom was hanging on my right ankle, and I pulled it back on. I set my bikini back up so that I was fully covered. I walked towards my clothes on the beach.

Miraculously, the beach was still quiet and deserted. The boys carried their suits back to the hotel. We went back to their penthouse. The three of us were exhausted, and I slept between them. I had a leg over Edmundo, and Ramiro slept with his hand between my thighs.

***

The next morning, I was delighted to wake up between them. Ramiro woke me up by rubbing my clit into an orgasm, the first of the day.

I opened my eyes. "Good morning."

Ramiro rolled me and pinned my shoulders to the mattress. "Good morning." He kissed me hard. He tasted like sin. He smelled like the best cologne money could buy. "Ready for round two?"

In response, I opened my legs and let my knees fall to the bed. Most runners weren't that flexible, but I was. My mom was a fanatic about me stretching, because she was a certified yoga instructor and she worried about the toll that running took on me.

Ramiro straightened out my legs, and he put them over his shoulders. He drove into my wetness, and I was wet enough to leave a spot on the sheets. I could feel my juices on my upper thighs. My feet were next to my ears, and he was pushing his shoulders against my calves and ankles.

I was helpless beneath him. He pushed me harder and harder, and I fell into my second orgasm of the day. I screamed as the force of my climax hit me like an oncoming semi.

He pulled out of me. Edmundo was definitely awake now.

"Get on your hands and knees." Edmundo put all the pillows under my stomach, and then he went behind me. I felt his hard cock graze my entrance, and I wanted it.

"Fuck me," I growled.

"Beg me."

"Please!" I pushed my hips back. "Please."

Edmundo slid an inch into me. "Is this what you want?"

"No!"

He slid out. "Oh?"

"More," I begged. "Please."

He pushed two inches into me, a little more than last time, but not enough, not nearly enough. "Is this it?"

"Fuck me!" I shouted. "All the way!"

He slammed into me, and I absorbed the force of his thrust with my hands on the mattress. It was hard enough to move me up the bed, towards Ramiro.

Ramiro was at my front, and now he was kneeling in front of me with his cock still wet with precum and my juices.

"Open wide." He was so big that I didn't think that I could fit him. My jaw dropped all it could, but he forced me even wider. He thrust roughly into my mouth. He pushed towards my throat, and I breathed through my gag reflex. As Edmundo pushed me forward, I took Ramiro deeper into my mouth. I normally used my hands and more finesse when I was giving a blow job, but I couldn't. My hands were otherwise occupied, and Ramiro was skull-fucking me.

He didn't last very long. He shot into my throat, and I swallowed almost everything. I couldn't get all of it, and some of it dribbled onto my cheeks and chin. He pulled out of me and backed away.

Edmundo took that as a cue to put his hand around the back of my neck and pin my head to the bed. He used his hand to pull me back onto him and push me forward with each thrust and retreat. He got faster and faster, and I couldn't do a thing. As I got closer, I arched my back.

I climaxed, and he shot into me. I loved feeling his hot cum fill my body.

He was still inside of me when he rolled us over. He was on his side, and I was his little spoon. He nibbled my earlobe.

"Ah, you are delicious."

"That was so good," I panted.

Ramiro was in front of me, and he kissed my nose. "How would you like to do this every day for the rest of your life?"

I smiled. "I'd love to, but I can't. I have a life to get back to. I have family that would miss me."

"What if we could fix that?" Ramiro looked straight into my eyes. "What if all of your obligations were taken care of, and you could live a life of luxury with us? What if we were your family and made one with you?"

"I'd love that. I'd love to bear your children. But it can't be true."

"It can." Edmundo flicked his fingers, and a perfect copy of me appeared. "Say the word, and your simulacrum will take your place. Nothing will be lost if you escape your life and stay with us." I could feel his cock getting bigger at the thought of keeping me forever and filling me with his baby.

I thought about it. What was left in my old life? Studying, getting a job, buying a house, marrying some guy, having 2.5 kids and a dog in a white-picket fenced house. That couldn't compare to the scorching hot offer of these two brothers. "Yes."

Edmundo pulled his dick out of me, and he pushed into my ass without stretching me before. He grunted as I cried out. Ramiro didn't waste any time, and he put my top leg over his as he thrust into me from the front. I was filled with both of them at the same time, and I was unbearably full. The two of them bit my shoulders, and the three of us climaxed.

"You are ours, now." Edmundo soothed his mark with his tongue. "You were made for us, to be our mate and bear our children."

EPILOGUE

I didn't freak out when they told me that they were dragons, but I was nervous when they said that they had to introduce me to the rest of the Brood. I shouldn't have been. When I got there, I saw Alice and Jade.

"Oh my god, you guys. What are you doing here?"

"We mated dragon shifters. You have, too."

"Wow."

"You ain't seen nothing yet, kid," Jade told me. She put her hand on my shoulder and half-turned me. Gabriella was sitting on a char. She waved.

"Oh my god! Gab!" I rushed forward and hugged her. "What? You're alive?"

"It was my simulacrum who died," she explained.

"But I watched you fall into the forest!"

"It was just an illusion," she said. "I chose a better life."

Alice and Jade agreed.

"We all did."

QUITO

LA DESPEDIDA

$\mathcal{I}$t was the night of our despedida from Ecuador. Those of us who went to PUCE-Quito were staying another week, but the ones who went to USFQ (San Francisco, out in Cayambe) were done with their semester. It was time for us to say goodbye before we went back to the normal grind back in the US. This summer, I had to study for the MCAT; a lot of my friends had GRE flashcards, and we all had things to do back home.

All of our host families came. They had reserved places with Esther the week before. It was a huge gathering, because everyone was there.

We gave the requisite speeches, and the program directors talked about how much they would miss our bright little faces. They went through all of this every semester, though, so it was hardly a new heartbreak.

At the end, we kissed our families goodbye. The students were going into a chiva that was chartered by the program for our despedida. With some food in our stomachs, we were going to bar crawl until we puked, and then we would keep going.

The chiva was basically a gigantic party bus. It had a disco ball and a bar stocked with more alcohol than even a few dozen college students could ever drink in one night. The Ecuadorian special was candela, which was cinnamon-laced liquor. The cinnamon helped it go down easier.

At the first stop, a tiny bar that none of us had ever been to, far away from La Mariscal, we got shots that the bartender set on fire. They were rainbow shots, with a bunch of different layers inside of them. We blew out the fire, and we drank. It was awesome to drink hot liquor, because of the way that it slid down your throat.

We didn't have adult supervision tonight, unless you counted our laid-back bus driver. He was used to driving a party bus, though. His main concern was driving us, and he didn't have to take care of us. We were adults, after all. So we had free rein to do whatever we wanted to do.

The second stop was an incredibly dark place. The bar in it was underground, and honestly it was pretty sketchy. There were a bunch of guys outside that kept shouting "CANNABIS" at us as the group of us hustled downstairs. It was packed from wall to wall with grinding bodies. The flashing red lights were the only illumination, and we fought our way through the dance floor to get to the bar. Alice sprung for a round of drinks for all of us, and we drank more.

I wasn't the kind of girl who did this. I barely drank in a normal semester, but tonight was a night for goodbyes. Tonight was a night for letting go. I worked my ass off normally, and it had served me well so far. But the wonderful thing about Ecuador was the way that I could let go and be someone who I wasn't. It didn't matter that the trains never ran on time here; it was all part of the journey.

After Jade threw up in the bus, the bus driver said that we would only get to do one more stop. We were responsible for cleaning up her vomit, but the driver told us that he didn't want to get any more puke in his vehicle. So we asked him to take us to Finn McCool's.

Finn McCool's was an Irish pub with gringo prices, but we went there every Tuesday anyway. They had a trivia night, and we had a huge group of us who played together. We won almost every week, by virtue of sheer numbers. All of our friends were some kind of teacher in the universities here. A lot of them were English teachers, but some of them taught upper-level biology and stuff. They were from Canada and the United States, and their lives were spent in pursuit of a good time. It was a kind of mild hedonism, but it was fascinating for me to see people who had their doctoral degrees just drink beer and chill in a dark pub with a ton of undergraduates.

They were not there tonight, though, because it was Friday. They were probably on a bar crawl of their own or at a house party; we'd done a few with them, but we didn't go every time that they called. The house parties always had new people, and sometimes the new people were really weird about Americans being there.

We descended on the largest table the instant that it was available, and it became ours. We ignored the disgusting stickiness of the table, and we piled our jackets everywhere. Quito gets cold at night.

I went to the bathroom, because my bladder couldn't handle the incredible fluid intake of this evening. The line was insanely long, because 5 of the other girls in my group came, too. Of course I took the last spot. There were a ton of Ecuadorian chicks there, too, and it was awful. At Finn McCool's, there was only one toilet in the ladies' room. I almost wanted to go into the guys' room, but because it was a Friday night, the guys' room would have plenty of action.

It was while staring the door that I saw him for the first time.

FIRST TIME

I'd seen a lot of men come out of the door at the Finn McCool's bathroom. The line was always long.

I had never seen a man like this.

He was tall, unbelievably tall, probably around 6' 5'. He had broad shoulders, and his face was dusted with freckles, the legacy of time spent in the sun. His hair was strawberry blond, and his lashes were auburn. They were long, long, long, the kind that would land you a job modeling for a cosmetics commercial or maybe a Latisse, a pharmaceutical focused on lengthening lashes, commercial.

He saw me looking at him.

"Hello."

His Irish accent was to die for. I was embarrassed to be caught looking at him, and it was hard for me to say anything. After a beat, where Jade in front of me turned around to give me a concerned look, I managed to say something.

"Hey." *Oh, goodness, I'm such a gauche American.*

He looked at the line of us, all of us obviously American.

"Having a girls' night out, then?"

"No," Jade interjected swiftly. "It's all girls. There are only girls in our program."

He smiled, slow and easy and somehow predatory.

"I think I can fix that. Where are you guys sitting?"

"Over in the back corner, at the banquet table."

"See you in a minute."

I looked at Jade, and we both shrugged. We had no idea what he meant, but if he wanted to join us, I would never get in his way. He was fine, the kind of guy who could grace magazine covers or be an Olympian. He had the broad shoulders of Michael Phelps with the kind of loose, confident walk that said that he was king.

Wow.

I heard Alice barfing inside of the bathroom.

"Oh my gosh, do you think she's ok?"

"She's fine." Jade shrugged. "I've already thrown up tonight, too. It comes with the territory." She reached into her purse. "That's why I carry mouthwash at all times." She showed me a tiny bottle of generic green mouthwash. "It's disgusting, but it gets the job done. Nobody likes the taste of puke in their mouth."

"You guys are way more experienced at this than I am." I shook my head. "I have no idea about that kind of stuff."

Jade laughed. "Nah, it's just what I learned during my crazy, wild phase. It's just a good idea to keep mouthwash you in general. You never know when your mouth could be absolutely foul."

The bathroom door opened, and Alice came out of there.

"Are you ok?"

"Yeah, I'm fine. I feel a lot better now, actually." Alice wiped her mouth with the back of her hand. "I'll go buy another round!" She walked off to talk to the bartender.

"Do you think that's wise?" I asked Jade. "I mean, we're already at the barfing stage."

"Don't worry about it." Jade was completely nonchalant. "We'll buy some food here, too."

She went into the bathroom, and she was in and out in less than a minute. I went, too, and I felt so much better after I splashed some water on my face. It wasn't good for my makeup, but it was good for me.

When I went out, I beelined for our table. I wasn't hungry yet, and I'd wait to order food as soon as I knew that we would be staying here. When I got there, I got a surprise.

RAINING MEN

There were chairs everywhere, and men were all over, chatting with all of us. I heard one of them tell Alice that he was a firefighter from Dana Point, near Los Angeles. From the looks of it, they were all tall, broad-shouldered, athletic men. It was like being in the Magic Mike movie, only it was real life. From the smiles on my friends' faces and how much they were laughing, it looked like the new additions were good company.

"Hi there," the gorgeous guy from the bathroom said. "I saved you a seat."

I blushed. I wasn't used to a lot of male attention. I'd never felt like I was a very pretty girl. I was curvy growing up, an early developer who had boobs when most girls were waiting to get their first periods. My dad was Jamaican, and my mom was white of Irish stock. From my dad, I got a mix of Afro-Jamaican and Chinese; from my mom I got the stockier build. All of my aunts were stacked like I was.

You could tell that I was mixed, but it was hard to figure out what kind of mixed I was. I loved the way that fellow Jamaican Tyson Beckford had shown people that it was cool to be exotic looking, but I didn't have the looks of a supermodel.

"Hi." I sat down on the chair next to him.

He tapped someone, a strawberry blond like him, on the shoulder. "She's here."

When he turned around, my breath caught.

IRISH TWINS

"*Y*ou're twins!"

"Yeah, but our mother loves us anyway." The second twin was smiling at me, and I closed my mouth. "What's your name, gorgeous?"

"Catie."

"Catherine, then, like the Duchess of Cambridge, wife of Prince William?"

"I don't know. My mom's Irish, so she named me Catie."

"Oh, really?" He looked at me. My skin didn't look Irish at all. "How interesting."

"My dad's Jamaican." When I was younger, the people who didn't believe that I was half Irish got me angry. I used to have screaming fights when I was in elementary school when people told me not to pretend. My mother, white as snow, was completely helpless in this situation, because she'd never dealt with racism in her life. My dad told me to let it go. I followed his advice now; I was used to it. It was part of being a multiracial person.

As a kid, I'd never felt very comfortable in my skin. I was a curvy kid, and I had acne during middle school and high school. I went to a zillion dermatologists to fix it, but they couldn't. I finally found a miracle product my senior year of high school that did what my antibiotics and prescription creams couldn't.

When I got to college, I'd suddenly become an attractive girl. It was really weird. I'd gone from no prom date in high school to having random guys walk up to me on the street to ask me for my number.

Like everything, I just got used to it. I gave them a fake number and moved one. Outright denying to give them my phone number never ended well. They would just end up following me down the sidewalk, whining, sort of like the creepy guys in that Hollaback video. It was a huge turn-off.

These guys were the polar opposite of college boys. They were much smoother, and they were a thousand times hotter, like a candle flame to the sun. The only way that I could tell them apart was by the clothes they were wearing. The first one I had met was wearing a navy blue polo shirt, and the second one was wearing forest green polo.

"That's really cool." He took a sip from his glass. "Could I buy you a drink?"

"Sure. I'll take a Blowjob."

It was a good thing that he'd already swallowed, because he would have sprayed everything everywhere. He sputtered, and then he started laughing uproariously, with his whole body.

He caught his breath. "What was that?"

"It's a shooter mixed drink made with Kahlua, Amaretto, and Bailey's Irish Cream topped with whipped cream." I'd never had one before I came to Finn McCool's, but it was my favorite drink to get here. "You don't use your hands to drink it."

"Done. I'll go grab two and some more pints." He got up and headed to the bar, moving effortlessly and gracefully through the throngs of people.

"What's your name?" I called in the crowded bar, across the music and chatter.

He turned and gave me a heart-stopping, panty-melting grin that show-cased his white, even teeth. "It's Ruari." He winked, and he walked forward again.

"Sorry about his manners," the second one said. "I'm Ultan. You should always introduce yourself before buying a girl a drink; our mother would be ashamed. It's just good manners."

"It's all right," I told him. "What brings you two to Ecuador."

"Oh, we're just on holiday really. We saved up the money to go around the world, and we started in Buenos Aires. We swung down to Tierra del Fuego and came up all the way through Chile. We went to Macchu Picchu and the Atacama Desert before coming to Ecuador. We stopped in Loja and Riobamba before staying in Quito, which actually has good Internet."

Ruari came back with our drinks. He was carefully holding four shots, two Blowjobs and two rainbow-colored shots.

"Two Blowjobs for you, and a shot a piece for us." He slid them on the table. "Cheers!"

"There's an Ecuadorian saying when you're doing a round of shots with friends." I picked up a Blowjob, completely ignoring the proper traditional consumption method. "Arriba, abajo, al centro, adentro. Above, below, to the center, inside."

"I think that's phenomenal." Ultan picked up a shot. "Let's do it, then. To friends!"

We chanted the four words, and we all drank our shots.

"Drink your second one," Ruari shouted across to me. "It looks good. Here's an Irish saying: 'Slainté'."

"Slainté!" I drank it up.

The two of them were looking at me like a cat looks at a delicious mouse.

PRIVATE

"Would you like to go somewhere more private?" Ultan put his hand on my knee.

In the normal course of things, I would have immediately peeled his hand off of my knee. I wasn't in the habit of letting complete strangers touch me.

But in Quito, tonight, I was a different person. I had had a lot to drink, but I was still capable of making my own decisions.

Looking between the two of them and their perfect faces, I threw caution to the wind.

"Let's go." I went over to Alice and shouted in her ear that I was leaving. She nodded, and she went back to talking to the scorching hot fireman.

I tried to go out the front, but Ruari pulled me back.

"We can't leave that way."

"Why not?"

The bouncer cut in. "We only offer the back door after hours, miss."

"Oh." I followed Ultan and Ruari to the back.

"Don't feel bad," Ultan shot over his shoulder. "I didn't know the first night at Finn McCool's, either. The bars in Quito have to respect a curfew, but they don't really abide by the law. They shutter their front door, but they still serve drinks and let people in and out of the back."

"I've been here a lot, though. I mean, I've never had to come out of the back." I looked around. "This is a really shady alley."

"Don't worry, lovely." Ruari swept the alley with his eyes. "You're safe with us. But we could get out of here."

"It's very late," Ultan said. "That's why Finn McCool's has different policies. Let's get a taxi."

We hailed a taxi. The taxi driver was charging us double as obvious foreigners, but it beat walking.

"Where are you going?"

"Calle Garcia Moreno and Calle Chile, please."

All of us were in very close quarters in the back. I was sandwiched between the two brothers. Their shoulders were very broad, and I scooted forward so that we'd all have enough room. I admired their muscular thighs discreetly. Their felt really good against mine, though I wasn't drunk enough to tell them that.

We were in the Centro Historico now, with loads of Spanish colonial architecture. It was very beautiful and very old, older than the United States. There were many good reasons why Quito had been named a UNESCO World Heritage Site. It was a hidden treasure, really. Iglesia de la Compania, the Jesuit church with everything covered in gold leaf, was absolutely beautiful. There was Moorish influence, as well, with the machihembra designs inside. There were old libraries in monasteries with books worth a fortune in Quito, but they were dusty and not that popular. Quito had a lot of secrets. Only a little had survived the turmoil in Ecuador over the years, but what remained was an echo of the Spanish colony that Ecuador had once been.

The taxi took us to the Hotel Grand Plaza. It was a gigantic hotel.

I was dazzled. "Isn't this where Hugo Chavez stays when he visits Ecuador? I think my literature professor, who also writes travel guides, said something to that effect."

"Yeah." Ruari was opening the door. "It is. We have the presidential suite."

HOTEL GRAND PLAZA

*U*ltan paid the cab driver, and Ruari put his arm around my waist. He squeezed me gently.

"Come on."

Ultan went past us, nodded at the doorman, and pushed into the hotel.

It was incredibly swanky, way more luxurious than anywhere I had ever been. I saw women dressed in evening gowns, the kind that you see on the red carpet. Because it's Ecuador, all of the gowns were probably hand-made. The men were all wearing at least suits and mostly tuxedoes.

I felt very underdressed here. Though Ruari and Ultan were dressed casually, too, they acted like it was nothing to move through a throng of expensively dressed people, the hoi aristoi of Latin America.

We got into the elevators, which were completely modern. Ultan pressed the button for the highest floor, and we zoomed up in no time at all.

"Would you like a drink?" Ultan gestured towards the sidebar, which had a variety of American beers and French wine bottles.

"I'm good, thanks."

"There's something that's been driving me crazy since you drank that second Blowjob."

"Oh?"

"This." Ruari's mouth crashed down on mine hard, with bruising force. He pulled back a little and licked the corner of my mouth. "You've had whipped cream there this whole time."

I didn't have time to be embarrassed though, because Ultan pulled me away from Ruari, spun me around, and leaned me back so that my back was parallel with the ground. He took my mouth in a hot, long, wet kiss. He smelled so good, and he tasted even better. Whatever was in those rainbow drinks was really good, or it was just Ultan.

His hand traveled to grab my butt, but he wasn't there just to squeeze me. He pulled me off the ground, then he launched us towards the bed, spinning so that he was on the bottom when we landed. I straddled him, and I rode him a little bit while we made out. It was hard to reach, though, because he was so tall.

I grabbed his collar to pull him upright, and we made out sitting up. Every moment of the kiss felt warm and right; my body felt like it was melting inside.

"You won't need these," Ruari whispered in my ear. He lifted my dress, and he ripped off my panties. I was really glad that I kept myself clean shaven because we went swimming so much.

"Arms up."

I lifted my arms, and Ruari stripped my dress off. I couldn't kiss Ultan anymore. He unsnapped my bra, and he pulled it off of me.

Ultan yanked me back, so that he could bite my throat hard. I'd have a hickey tomorrow, but I didn't care. It felt so good when he bit me, like eating chocolate gelato and driving a race car at the same time. My heart rate was fast.

Ruari pushed me forward, and Ultan wasn't biting me anymore. He was flat on his back, and I pulled at his pants to get them off. I couldn't bear for him to be clothed for another second. I finally got the button open, and I unzipped it. He arched as he took off his shirt.

We were skin to skin now, covered in sweat from the heat of our passion. He had a hand on his dick, and he was guiding it to my entrance. I used my hands to push myself down onto him. He stretched me wide, so wide. My mouth dropped open, and I stopped moving.

"Can you take more?" Without waiting for a response from me, he pulled me down another inch with a firm hand on the back of my neck. He had more to give. He kept pulling me down — with each instant, I thought I couldn't take anymore, but he kept giving it to me anyway. I felt like I was split in two pieces around him.

I loved it. He was touching me where no man had ever touched me inside. I wasn't a virgin, but he had the widest, hardest dick I'd ever had.

I felt something cold touch my asshole. I yelped, and I pushed myself up. I was about to pull myself off of Ultan when he held my shoulders.

"Stay."

"I've never done anal before."

"It'll be good." He kissed me tenderly on the mouth, an open-mouthed kiss. "You'll see."

I let my torso fall back onto his. His hand swept down my back, soothing me. My hair was falling everywhere.

Ruari went back to slicking me up. He wasn't just touching my ass. He was rubbing me slowly at my sacrum and my taint, and it felt really good. I could feel his finger stretching my little hole, sliding in with the cold lube, which was quickly warming up. He stretched me more and more. My glutes clenched around him, and he stopped.

"Breathe."

I tried to relax, but it was hard. I'd never done anything like this before.

Ultan knew how to fix it, though. With one hand on my neck, he moved me up and down on him. I fluttered wildly around him, and the tension in my body eased. Ruari was able to slip in two fingers with the rhythm that Ultan was setting. I felt them both sliding into me.

Suddenly, Ruari's fingers weren't there anymore. Something much bigger was pushing into me.

I moaned, and I bit Ultan's shoulder with the intensity that I felt while being double penetrated. Ultan was big, and Ruari was the same size.

Ruari didn't stop. He put his hand lightly around my throat as he pushed me towards his dick.

It burned to have him in there, but there was pleasure, too. It was a good thing that there was lube to begin with.

They started moving, with my body sandwiched between them. They set a demanding rhythm, and I held on for the wild ride.

I heard Ultan moan, and he bucked wildly into my body. He shot hot cum into me, which triggered my orgasm. I climaxed hard around him.

Ruari picked up the pace. He rammed into me so hard that the headboard knocked into the wall with each thrust. I'd never had anal sex before, but he wasn't being gentle with me. It was violent, hard thrusting as he shot spurt after spurt of hot cum into my body. He bit my shoulder as he climaxed.

DRINKS

*R*uari collapsed onto my body, and we all lay there. We needed to catch our breaths, to breathe, after the mind-blowing orgasms we'd just had.

Ruari pulled out of my ass, and Ultan twisted so that I was on my side. Ruari got off the bed.

"We're going to be traveling for a while. Do you want to come with us?"

"Going where?"

"We're heading to New Zealand next. If you want, it won't cost a thing. Just stay with us."

"Yes. I'll stay with you." Ultan kissed me.

Ruari had three wine glasses with red wine in them. "Nothing like a drink after an orgasm."

I thought it was kind of weird, but I also wasn't going to say anything to someone who I'd just had sex with. "Ok." I accepted the glass that he gave me. I drank it.

"Is there honey in this wine? It's so sweet."

"No, there's no honey in it." Ultan and Ruari drank their own.

Ruari climbed back into bed with the two of us. We were covered in sweat and our juices, but I felt so tired. They must have been, too, because it was lights out for all of us. I snuggled with both of them as I drifted off.

MORNING LIGHT

When I woke up, there was the tantalizing scent of freshly baked bread and bacon.

"Good morning, sunshine."

When I opened my eyes, there was a whole spread of food just waiting to be eaten. I was sticky, but I went and picked up a slice of bacon. It was crisp, warm, and salty.

"Yum."

"What are your plans for today?"

"I don't know." I shrugged. "I guess I should call my host mom to tell her that I'm alive. She's pretty chill about me staying out with my friends, though. I tend to sleep it over at people's houses, so she won't worry or anything. I'll text her." I stood, and I went to my purse. I bent to get my phone out, and I felt Ruari stand behind me with an erection.

"Hold that thought. I have to text her." I scribbled something fast in Spanish — my phone was so basic that I actually *used* T9 — and I let it fall back into my purse.

I turned around, and I let Ruari kiss me with the kind of scorching kiss that he was so good at.

"There's something we have to tell you, if you're traveling with us."

"What is it?" Please don't let them be axe murderers.

"We're dragons." Ruari backed up a little bit, and he shifted his hand into a very big claw.

"Oh my god." I stumbled back so that my back was flat against the wall. "Oh my god."

"It's not a big deal." Ruari pressed against my body. "It just means that we have long lives. You will, too, since we've mated you."

"Mated me? Do you mean had sex?"

"We bit you. You've had our blood. You're ours now."

"I don't have time for this." I shook my head. "I have to go back and spend my summer studying for the MCAT. I have to go to medical school. I don't have the time to have dragon shifters as mates."

"Don't worry." Ultan came over, too. "We'll send back a copy of you to live the life you would have lead if you weren't our fated mate. Look." He flicked his fingers, and a full-sized clone of me was there, fully dressed in last night's clothes. She picked up my purse, and she walked out the door like it was nothing.

"Stay." Ruari nuzzled my throat and kissed it. "Stay."

"Ok," I whispered.

Ultan came in, and the three of us were close together. One.